FICTION HOUSE PRESS
PRESENTS

PRIVATE EYE

November 1959
Vol. 1, No. 1

This reprint edition is a facsimile of the original pulp magazine. Variations in printing and quality can be attributed to the original magazine which was printed on rough woodpulp paper. No attempt has been made to politically correct any language deemed inappropriate to the modern reader.

New Material
© 2021 Fiction House Press

ISBN 978-1-64720-249-1

www.FictionHousePress.com
fictionhousepress@gmail.com

Make More Money in One of Today's FASTEST-GROWING Industries

We'll train and establish you in
YOUR OWN LIFETIME BUSINESS

U.S. Dept. of Commerce says— 45 million homes in U.S. with...

$750 million yearly potential in rug and upholstery cleaning...

In your town, just 2 jobs a day earn $8,750 profit first year...

You become an independent business man with financial and social success.

Big Future in Dynamic Industry

Join the thousands of opportunity-minded men like those pictured below who are sharing in the profits that this remarkable home-furnishings cleaning field makes possible. We can help you make more money in a booming industry which the Dept. of Commerce estimates as having a $750 million dollar a year potential!

We will train you as a cleaning specialist, show you the proven methods for building business, and work with you providing over 27 continuous services that help assure your growth.

Arlis Wilson of Tulsa says: "As a Duraclean Dealer I have the ideal setup. I am operating my own business, yet have at my disposal a staff of experienced men at Headquarters who will help me on a moment's notice."

We Help Build Your Business

YOUR personal success is of the utmost importance to Headquarters, for as you grow so grows the Duraclean Dealer organization. Thus, your initial training is only the beginning of a continuous assistance program designed to build your business. When you contact Hdqtrs. you receive prompt, expert counsel from a staff of specialists. Some of the over 27 services you receive are conventions and regional conferences, new product development, trademark protection, sales letters, tested ads, local promotional materials, a monthly sales-building magazine, plus a host of others.

Backed by National Advertising

You are backed by a National Advertising program which is larger than all other similar programs in the industry combined. **Consumer Advertising:** Ads dramatizing Duraclean services reach millions through leading magazines as *McCalls, Parents', House & Garden, House Beautiful, Canadian Homes & Gardens, Sunset, New Yorker* and others. **Trade Advertising:** More and more retailers are turning over customers to Duraclean Dealers for servicing. Key trade magazines as *Interiors, Floor Covering Profits, Furniture Retailer, Cleaning & Laundry Age,* are a few of many used in targeting local retailers to become your agents.

What Dealers Say

W. Lookiebill (St. Louis): My 28th year! Began during depression and built business on good service.

D. Chilcott (N. Platte): Duraclean say gross $9.00 per hour. I gross up to $12.00. Many dealers do much better.

M. Lyons (Chgo): 3rd year should hit $100,000; 2nd was $60,000; 1st $40,000. Hdqrs help make it possible.

E. Roddey (Hampton, Va.): Did $600.00 first 12 days in January. My business keeps growing each month.

Start Part-Time If Employed

Even if you are now employed, you may start enjoying the financial independence of your OWN business. Many dealers start part-time, and as they expand their operation beyond what they can service on a sparetime basis, they switch to full-time. Later they expand further by hiring servicemen. This could be your pattern for success.

You will receive local training with an established dealer and at our 5-day, 50-hour factory training school. Thus, under our guidance, you become an expert in the care of rugs and upholstery, a profession for which there is now great demand.

Alert dealers can gross $9.00 hourly, plus $6.00 on each serviceman at national price scale. You enjoy big profits on both materials and labor. Everything furnished to get you started.

Six Ways to Make Money

A Duraclean Dealership qualifies you to offer six different services. Thus on many jobs you multiply profits.
1. **Duraclean:** Unique ABSORPTION process for cleaning and reviving rugs, carpets, upholstery. Recommended by leading stores and manufacturers. No scrubbing, soaking, shrinkage. Aerated foam manufactured by portable electric Foamovator safely removes dirt, grease, unsightly spots. Dries so fast customers use furnishings in a few hours.
2. **Durashield:** *Soil-retarding* treatment that KEEPS furnishings clean MONTHS longer. Applied after cleaning, this invisible film protects each fiber from dirt.
3. **Duraproof:** Protects against damage by moths, carpet beetles. Only such treatment backed by 6-year Warranty!
4. **Duraguard:** A flame-proofing treatment which reduces fire damage by retarding charring and tendency of fires to flame up. Theaters, restaurants, hotels, homes, offer huge potential.
5. **Spotcraft:** Special chemical products which enable you to handle most all spot or staining problems.
6. **Carpet Repair:** Special tools and know-how equip you to provide this specialized service.

Easy Terms

A moderate payment establishes your own business— pay balance from sales. We furnish electric machines, folders, store cards and enough materials to return your TOTAL investment. You can have your business operating in a few days. Mail coupon today!

NO STAMP OR ENVELOPE NEEDED

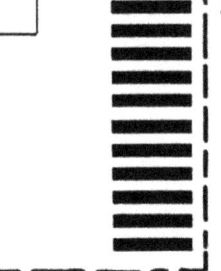

Cut out & mail this postage-paid card for FREE 16-Page BOOKLETS!

Write your name and address at top of card and mail. No obligation. No salesman will call. You get FREE illustrated booklets which tell how you can enjoy steadily increasing lifetime income in YOUR OWN BUSINESS.

DURACLEAN COMPANY
9-74N Duraclean Bldg., Deerfield, Ill.

FROM:
YOUR NAME..
ADDRESS..
CITY...............ZONE....STATE...........

No Postage Stamp Necessary If Mailed in the United States

BUSINESS REPLY CARD
First Class Permit No. 3, Deerfield, Illinois

POSTAGE WILL BE PAID BY

DURACLEAN COMPANY
9-74N Duraclean Bldg.
Deerfield, Illinois

Private Eye

VOL. 1 NO. 1 NOV

Hunt Grenfall
 EDITORIAL DIRECTOR
Sol R. Brodsky
 ART DIRECTOR
Hank Baligossio
 MANAGING EDITOR
Arthur Jenners
Harriet Belkan
 ASSOCIATE EDITORS
Sally Finkel
 ASSISTANT EDITOR
Garr Tindall
 PICTURE EDITOR
Milton Simon
 ART EDITOR

PRIVATE EYE is published by CAL-YORK Features, Inc., 24 West 45th Street, New York 36, N. Y. Application to mail at second-class postage rates is pending at New York, N. Y. and Canton, Ohio. Single copy price: 35 cents. Subscription rate $2.00 a year. Not responsible for loss or non-return of manuscripts, photographs or illustrations. And all material must be accompanied by stamped, self-addressed envelope.
Entire contents copyright 1959. Names of characters used in fiction and semi-fiction material are fictitious and any resemblance to persons living or dead is purely coincidental.
Advertising representative: Ray Peck Associates, 545 Fifth Avenue, New York 17, N. Y. Printed in USA.
CREDITS: Page 13, Photo by Ed Berger.

CONTENTS

ACTION

SING A SONG OF SEX-MAIL 10
 Star sleuth Adam Baxter gets involved with blackmail, an oddball client and 2 strange blondes.

DANGEROUS CURVES 13
 Curvaceous but brainy Liz Hunter finds thrills and threats in the world's most dangerous profession.

RED MEANS BLOOD 20
 ...and plenty of it.... when foreign agents try to frame Mark Randall and almost make it!

BOSOMS AND BULLETS 36
 The most "offbeat" private eye ever, battles 2 lovely, deadly sisters. The background is Greenwich Village.

FACT THRILLER

BARKER-KARPIS GANG 25
 Meet "Ma" Barker and Alvin Karpis: the most evil twosome in the history of American Crime.

EXPOSÉ

I SMASHED THE VICE PHOTO RACKET 30
 A camera can be a vicious instrument for depravity or perversion. What this sleuth found out...

SPECIAL BONUS

MESSAGE OF MURDER 39
 STARRING ADAM BAXTER. Our Big Story introduces our top sleuth in a wild chase and wilder women.

PIC FEATURES

TV PRIVATE EYES 16
 The mystery fan has a field day with the gangland shows and ace "private 'I's'". This month we are starring "77 Sunset Strip."

FOLLOW THOSE GIRLS 22
 Take a look at the gals and you'll see what we mean.

GAL FRIDAY TO A PRIVATE EYE 34
 All work and some play makes an exciting career for a sleuth steno, Monica March.

"PRIVATE EYE" EXTRAS

YOU BE A PRIVATE EYE 33
 Test your talents—see if you can solve this case.

P'EYE'S CARTOONS 29
 A couple of howls by Don Oreheck and Bill Riley.

MISS PRIVATE EYE 28
 Meet some of the glamorous gals who want to win our "Curve Caper Contest".

How to pass a genius

All of us can't be geniuses. But any ordinarily talented mortal can be a success—and that's more than some geniuses are.

Now, as in Æsop's time, the race doesn't always go to the one who potentially is the swiftest. The *trained* man has no trouble in passing the genius who hasn't improved his talents.

In good times and bad times, in every technical and business field, the *trained* man is worth a dozen untrained ones, no matter how gifted.

The International Correspondence Schools can't make you into a genius. For more than 67 years, however, I. C. S. has been helping its students to become *trained, successful leaders*—and it can do the same for you.

Mark your special interest on the coupon. Don't be like the unsuccessful genius who wastes his life in dreaming of what he intends to do. *Act* now!

For Real Job Security—Get an I. C. S. Diploma! I. C. S., Scranton 15, Penna. Accredited Member, National Home Study Council

---

INTERNATIONAL CORRESPONDENCE SCHOOLS — ICS

BOX 59545-J, SCRANTON 15, PENNA. (Partial list of 258 courses)

Without cost or obligation, send me "HOW to SUCCEED" and the opportunity booklet about the field BEFORE which I have marked X (plus sample lesson):

ARCHITECTURE and BUILDING CONSTRUCTION
- Air Conditioning
- Architecture
- Arch. Drawing and Designing
- Building Contractor
- Building Estimator
- Carpenter Builder
- Carpentry and Millwork
- Carpenter Foreman
- Heating
- Painting Contractor
- Plumbing
- Reading Arch. Blueprints

ART
- Commercial Art
- Magazine Illus.
- Show Card and Sign Lettering
- Sketching and Painting

AUTOMOTIVE
- Automobile
- Auto Body Rebuilding and Refinishing
- Auto Engine Tuneup
- Auto Technician

AVIATION
- Aero-Engineering Technology
- Aircraft & Engine Mechanic

BUSINESS
- Accounting
- Advertising
- Business Administration
- Business Management
- Cost Accounting
- Creative Salesmanship
- Managing a Small Business
- Professional Secretary
- Public Accounting
- Purchasing Agent
- Salesmanship
- Salesmanship and Management
- Traffic Management

CHEMICAL
- Analytical Chemistry
- Chemical Engineering
- Chem. Lab. Technician
- Elements of Nuclear Energy
- General Chemistry
- Natural Gas Prod. and Trans.
- Petroleum Prod. and Engr.
- Professional Engineer (Chem)
- Pulp and Paper Making

CIVIL ENGINEERING
- Civil Engineering
- Construction Engineering
- Highway Engineering
- Professional Engineer (Civil)
- Reading Struc. Blueprints
- Sanitary Engineer
- Structural Engineering
- Surveying and Mapping

DRAFTING
- Aircraft Drafting
- Architectural Drafting
- Drafting & Machine Design
- Electrical Drafting
- Mechanical Drafting
- Sheet Metal Drafting
- Structural Drafting

ELECTRICAL
- Electrical Engineering
- Elec. Engr. Technician
- Elec. Light and Power
- Practical Electrician
- Practical Lineman
- Professional Engineer (Elec)

HIGH SCHOOL
- High School Diploma
- Good English
- High School Mathematics
- High School Science
- Short Story Writing

LEADERSHIP
- Industrial Foremanship
- Industrial Supervision
- Personnel-Labor Relations
- Supervision

MECHANICAL and SHOP
- Diesel Engines
- Gas-Elec. Welding
- Industrial Engineering
- Industrial Instrumentation
- Industrial Metallurgy
- Industrial Safety
- Machine Shop Practice
- Mechanical Engineering
- Professional Engineer (Mech)
- Quality Control
- Reading Shop Blueprints
- Refrigeration and Air Conditioning
- Tool Design
- Tool Making

RADIO, TELEVISION
- General Electronics Tech.
- Industrial Electronics
- Practical Radio-TV Eng'r'g
- Practical Telephony
- Radio-TV Servicing

RAILROAD
- Car Inspector and Air Brake
- Diesel Electrician
- Diesel Engr. and Fireman
- Diesel Locomotive

STEAM and DIESEL POWER
- Combustion Engineering
- Power Plant Engineer
- Stationary Diesel Engr.
- Stationary Fireman

TEXTILE
- Carding and Spinning
- Cotton Manufacture
- Cotton Warping and Weaving
- Loom Fixing Technician
- Textile Designing
- Textile Finishing & Dyeing
- Throwing
- Warping and Weaving
- Worsted Manufacturing

Name_____ Age_____ Home Address_____

City_____ Zone_____ State_____ Working Hours_____ A.M. to P.M._____

Occupation_____

Canadian residents send coupon to International Correspondence Schools, Canadian, Ltd., Montreal, Canada. ... Special low monthly tuition rates to members of the U. S. Armed Forces.

PRIVATE EYE shoots off its mouth

A Talk with our readers

As the Editors of PRIVATE EYE, we'd like to use this space to introduce ourselves to our readers. To explain as briefly as possible what our aims and objectives are. Perhaps in this way we can become better acquainted, and it is our hope that this acquaintanceship will grow into a lasting friendship through the issues and years ahead.

Right off, we'd like to go down on record as saying that the first and most important objective of any magazine is to *entertain*! We also want to say that as the editors of PRIVATE EYE we have dedicated ourselves to this objective. Of course, entertainment is not one thing. It has to be many things or it soon becomes dull. If, as they say, that variety is the spice of life, then we at PRIVATE EYE believe that the *life* of a magazine depends on *variety*. And that is exactly what PRIVATE EYE offers its readers, a variety of carefully selected subjects related to the exciting field of *detection* and *law enforcement*. Suppose we take these subjects up one at a time and show you what we mean.

Let's begin with *Adam Baxter*, one of the most interesting subjects you're likely to meet in many a moon. Adam Baxter typifies the *private investigator* at his very best. The key word behind Adam Baxter is action—fast, furious and flavorful. A man's man (and a gal's man too) you'll find the Adam Baxter adventure a balanced mixture of taut-drama, high-level suspense along with a pace guaranteed to keep you panting to the final exclamation point.

In the category of *Police Case Histories* we offer the *Barker-Karpis Gang*. Their rise to notoriety, and their do-or-die battle against J. Edgard Hoover's fabulous F. B. I.

For the reader who likes sleuthing we have provided an illustrated, mystifying case history. Here is a chance to test your detective skills. If you find yourself stumped, the solution will be found elsewhere in the mag.

There is also a TV section. Here, and in future issues, we will bring you the big names in the world of TV, and movie crime detection and law enforcement programs. We will also offer "sneak-previews" of new shows dealing with the "private-eye," and according to one informant great things are shaping up in this direction.

As we said a couple of paragraphs back, entertainment was the one important objective a magazine should strive for. We also said that entertainment was variety. As one of these variations, and in a most stimulating manner, we've included a Photo-Story featuring *Liz Hunter*, our *Private Eye-Ful*. We think you'll like "Liz". On second thought, we don't have to think about it. We *know* you'll like her.

Since objectives have a way of reaching out into the future, we don't want to forget to tell you what lies ahead.

As the editors of PRIVATE EYE, our plans are to bring you, our readers, the very best in detective reading. Arrangements with the country's top authors have already been made as part of our program to make PRIVATE EYE just about the best detective magazine on the stands today.

If you have a preference for a certain kind of story, let us know. If you have a gripe, then sound off. It's only by knowing your interests that we can serve you better. Or maybe it's information you're after. If it's related in any way to detective or police enforcement activities we'll do our best to get the info for you. That's why we've included a "Question and Answer" department — just for this purpose.

To sum it up, it's been a lot of work, but also fun, wrapping up this first issue of PRIVATE EYE. We hope you like the package. It comes to you with our sincere wishes for the best reading ever.

Sincerely,

The Editors

* Private Eye

THIS is how you train at home to become a SERVICE ENGINEER in the Air Conditioning and Refrigeration industry...

25 BIG KITS

An old industry offers bright new opportunities

Almost any industry has jobs for men with special skills. In many cases, good pay and steady work are the rule. Yet—would you be happy in being a repairman all your life? Wouldn't you rather have a job that presents a *challenge*—still *bigger* money—an opportunity to *grow?*

Listen, if you are ambitious to *keep climbing:* The air conditioning and refrigeration industry is growing so fast that 20,000 newly-trained technicians are needed each year. They can come only from the technical schools. Because installation and repair work is important, graduates may expect high pay and security right from the start. That's not all. *A well-trained technician has a great opportunity to develop into a Service Engineer.* As a matter of fact, 90 percent of all refrigeration engineers are former repairmen!

If you seek a *career*, not just a job, get into air conditioning and refrigeration. Your first step is to gain skill and knowledge. Learn at home by practicing with 25 big kits that CTI sends. Acquire experience as you train.

CTI ships you all parts and tools—with shop-proved instruction—to build a heavy-duty, commercial-type, ¼ h.p. condensing unit (illustrated above.) You complete 23 field-type projects—do 10 trouble-shooting jobs. You make home a training center!

So practical is CTI training that many students earn extra cash in spare time soon after they start. They make calls on their own, or get part-time jobs with local appliance dealers or air conditioning contractors.

But read the complete story. It is told in a new CTI catalog. *Just fill out and mail coupon below for your copy.* Sample lesson included. No cost nor obligation—Commercial Trades Institute, Chicago 26, Ill.

```
┌─────────────────────────────────────────────────────┐
│ COMMERCIAL TRADES INSTITUTE                         │
│ 1400 GREENLEAF AVENUE                               │
│ CHICAGO 26, ILLINOIS                    DEPT. R-633 │
│ Send catalog, Success in Air Conditioning & Refrigeration, and │
│ Lesson Sample. Both FREE.                           │
│                                                     │
│ Name_____ Age_____    │
│                                                     │
│ Address_____        │
│                                                     │
│ City_____ Zone___ State_____   │
└─────────────────────────────────────────────────────┘
```

PRIVATE EYE PREVIEWS

By Fernando West

Each issue we will preview what we believe will interest you whether it be Television, Movies, books or any other medium with a police, private detective or adventure theme. To the mystery fan—the best of seasons is coming up!

ABC television has come up with a new show breaking this Fall that promises lots of action and excitement. It stars a name that has been popular in the movies for a long time. Robert Taylor. The title of the series as we go to press is "Robert Taylor's Detectives."

Mr. Taylor will be seen in the role of Police Captain Matt Holbrook, a brilliant criminal investigator.

The series features Lee Farr as Lt. James Conway, Tigre Andrews as Lt. John Russo and Russell Thorsen as Lt. Otto Lindstrom.

This looks like a real colorful series with lots of interesting cases and characters. If you follow the police programs, then this is one we heartily recommend.

Another television show coming up is one based on Raymond Chandler's famed private-eye "Philip Marlowe."

"Marlowe" recreates the adventures of a tough detective who moves with equal ease from the world of squealers, ne'er do wells and double-crossers to the preserves of socialites, fast-buck pirates and moneyed hipocrites.

This again is real suspense and thrilling action. The title role will be played by Phillip Carey, and makes its debut in the early Fall on the ABC Television network.

POINT ??? ??? BLANK

Questions and Answers

To the Editor:

A friend and I have both wondered where the word *cop* comes from. My friend thinks it comes from the German, but I think it might've come from the French. Anyway, which one of us would be right?

Ernie Clark
Dayton, Ohio

Neither! The word comes from the English phrase, Constable On Patrol. By combining the first letter of each of these words, the word 'cop' was originated.

*

To the Editor:

I once heard that certain kinds of crimes happened more often at certain times of the year. Would this actually be a fact?

Robert Spivak
Ann Arbor, Mich.

Definitely. According to F.B.I. reports, crime patterns do follow the seasons. In the winter robberies will show an increase, whereas in the summer, homicide and assault will outnumber other crimes. In the late fall larceny heads the list. It might sound screwy, but there's no arguing with statistics.

*

To the Editor:

I've often wondered how large the nation's police force actually is. Would there be as many as a quarter of a million policemen?

Michael Jenks
Muskegon, Michigan

You're way over, Mike. The 40,000 police jurisdictional areas in the United States are staffed by some 175,000 policemen. This is as of 1950 and includes part-time as well as fully employed law officers.

*

To the Editor:

It must take a lot of money to run the F.B.I. How much does it cost us taxpayers to keep the G-MEN going?

Harry Last
Ft. Worth, Texas

This will come as a surprise, but the F.B.I. is actually running at a profit. Since 1924 the cost of operation was $983,179,840. But during this same period, the Agency collected both in fines and by recoveries, a total of $1,390,093,138. Substract the two and you'll find a plump profit of over 400 million!

*

Send your questions to:
POINT BLANK, Calyork Features, Inc.,
24 West 45th Street, New York 36, N. Y.

"YOU ARE UNDER ARREST"

There's a Thrill in Bringing a Crook to Justice Through Scientific
CRIME DETECTION!

We have taught thousands of men and women this exciting, profitable pleasant profession. Let us teach you, too, *in your own home*. Prepare yourself in your leisure time, to fill a responsible, steady, well-paid position in a very short time and at very small cost. What others have done, you, too, can do.

Be A FINGER PRINT Expert

Over 800 Bureaus of Identification In the U.S. Now Employ I.A.S. Trained Men as Directors or Assistants

Here's a Partial List of Them

Send for FREE Complete list of over 800 Bureaus where our Students or Graduates are now working

State Bureau of Michigan
Tallahassee, Florida
State Bureau of Connecticut
State Bureau of Arizona
State Bureau of Rhode Island
Charleston, S. C.
State Bureau of Louisiana
State Bureau of Utah
Lincoln, Nebraska
Trenton, New Jersey
Albany, New York
Dayton, Ohio
Stillwater, Oklahoma
Montgomery, Alabama
Phoenix, Arizona
Santa Ana, Calif.
Seattle, Washington
Madison, Wisconsin
Miami, Florida
Leavenworth, Kansas
Annapolis, Maryland
Dearborn, Michigan
Vicksburg, Miss.
Hartford, Connecticut
San Juan, Porto Rico
Ketchikan, Alaska
Honolulu, Hawaii

Not Expensive or Difficult to Learn at Home

Scientific Crime Detection is inexpensive to learn. It's a thrilling occupation for which you can train in your spare time. It's a science —a real science, which when mastered THROUGH HOME STUDY TRAINING gives you something no one can EVER take from you. As long as you live you should be able to make good in scientific crime detection. "We will teach you Finger Print Identification— Firearms Identification—Police Photography—and Criminal Investigation." That's what we told the men who now handle those jobs in Identification Bureaus. And now we repeat, but THIS time it's to YOU... Just give us a chance and we'll train you to fill a good position in the fascinating field of scientific crime detection.

NOW IS THE TIME TO START!

New Bureaus of Identification are being established right along. Naturally, the need for more well trained Finger Print Experts is evident. Fit yourself now to hold down a fine job as a recognized technician in Crime Detection. You can learn this fascinating profession in your own home and you can pay as you learn.

FREE! "BLUE BOOK OF CRIME"

It's a thriller, filled from cover to cover with exciting information on scientific crime detection. It tells about some of the most interesting crimes, and how the criminals were brought to justice through the very methods which you are taught in the I. A. S. course. You can get started on this important training, at low cost, and without delay. The book will tell you how. Don't wait. Clip the coupon and send it along TODAY. No salesman will call.

INSTITUTE OF APPLIED SCIENCE
(A Correspondence School Since 1916)
Dept. 1596   1920 Sunnyside Ave., Chicago 40, Ill.

Clip and Mail Coupon Now

INSTITUTE OF APPLIED SCIENCE
Dept 1596   1920 Sunnyside Ave., Chicago 40, Ill.

Gentlemen: Without obligation, send me the "Blue Book of Crime," and complete list of over 800 Identification Bureaus employing your students or graduates, together with your low prices and Easy Terms Offer. No salesman will call.

Name..
Address....................RFD or Zone..........
City..................State..........Age.....

ACTION

Adam Baxter

PRIVATE EYE

If I stood still I was a dead duck. I dived for the bed and started swinging.

SING A SONG OF SEX-MAIL

I thought he was just another rich old geezer who'd gotten into a blackmail jam. Then I found out about the secrets he and his young nympho wife shared.

SING A SONG OF SEX-MAIL

I KNEW I HAD A CLIENT the moment I saw the shadow of a man etched against the frosted glass panel in my office door. Whoever it was outside in the hall paused and fiddled around, reading the gilt lettering "Adam Baxter, Private Investigator" at ⁻⁺ a dozen times. That's a sure sign of a customer—
problems.

⁻d waited. Then the old geezer opened the
⁻⁻de. I saw that he was nervous and

⁻lid my feet off my desk,
⁻⁻ was about 58 or
was the kind
⁻t who is
⁻ving

"I—that is—a friend of mine suggested..."
The balding moneybags was having himself a hell of a bad time. He stammered and stuttered and diddled with his expensive gloves and hat. I let him stew in his own juice a little and then nodded him into a chair.

"My—my name is J. Henderson Willoughby," he said. I whistled to myself. J. Henderson was a well-known man about town, a multi-millionaire financier, sportsman and pillar of the community. I riffled through my brain-box index file and remembered that I'd recently read a story that he'd separated from his wife—a real high society figure.

"Okay, Mr. Willoughby," I grunted. "What is it? You want me to check up on your wife—or is someone blackmailing you?"

(Continued on next page)

SING A SONG OF SEX-MAIL

He looked shocked and surprised. I told him that I couldn't imagine any other reason why he would find it necessary to visit a private eye on a cold rainy afternoon. He inhaled deeply, shook his head and made a gesture that indicated that he was ready to spill all his troubles.

"It's—well, it *is* blackmail," he began.

THE STORY WAS JUST about what I would have figured. Like many men of his income bracket and age, J. Henderson Willoughby had wanted to sow some last wild oats before his hormones gave out altogether. His choice for a playmate had been Annette Dahl, a redheaded, 22-year-old sexboat who warbled second-rate blues songs in a third-rate nightclub.

J. Henderson had fallen the way only an aging millionaire can tumble. He'd set Annette up in an apartment with all the trimmings—Caddy, minks, diamonds, the works.

Willoughby had been "visiting" Annette in her swank apartment about three, maybe four, times a week—all his fading metabolism could take. He and she had shed lots of inhibitions together during his "visits."

Unfortunately—and unknown to J. Henderson—someone had evidently rented the apartment next door. Using all the old gimmicks—mike under the bed and a hole cut in the wall behind a one-way-glass mirror—some sharp hoods had collected a big batch of sizzling words and pictures of the millionaire and the doll making hay—in the hay.

I hit her across the face—once, twice, three times.

"Hold it!" I froze. The voice was a man's—

"Two men came to my office yesterday, Mr. Baxter," Willoughby went on. "They brought—well, prints of the photographs and copies of the tape recordings. They showed me the pictures and played the tapes—and they said they wanted $250,000 within 72 hours!"

"Or else?" I asked.

"Or else they'd turn the things over to my wife—and my business associates," he replied. "With the photos and tapes, my wife could demand—and get—millions as an alimony settlement if she went through with a divorce. As far as my business associates are concerned, the disaster would be even worse. I'd be ruined—and totally disgraced in society!"

I could imagine what was on the tapes—and what the camera lens had caught. When a character like moneybags Willoughby takes a flier at sex and sin, he usually goes for the more exotic and bizarre nuances of the lovemaking.

"Okay," I shrugged. "I suppose you want me to take the case—and get back the negatives and all the tapes without the cops knowing anything about it?"

"Yes."

"It'll cost you," I declared. "I want $2,500 as a retainer —$10,000 more if I pull it off."

The check for the $2,500 was in my hand, the ink still wet, a minute later. I waved it dry, took out a pencil and a pad and spent the next half hour asking Willoughby a lot of questions—names, addresses...

At 2:55 p.m., I was in his bank, getting the check cashed. I shoved the C-notes and fifties into my inside coat pocket—and got to work.

I HAD A DAY AND A HALF before the ultimatum the blackmailers had given Willoughby would be up. They'd told him they'd telephone him and tell him where to meet them with the cash. I knew damn well that it would be useless to try and spring a trap. The gang wouldn't have the negatives and tapes along. I could be sure of that. The crooks had hold of a good thing—and they doubtless intended milking the millionaire for plenty. The $250,000 was only their first bite! *(Continued)*

DANGEROUS CURVES

When they called in Hollywood's sexiest detective, it wasn't for a part in a new movie. This was a real life caper to uncover the scheme of a dame and her underworld boy friends. It was a battle of shapes and action... with both babes giving their all, and that was plenty.

* Private Eye

"We need someone with guts, brains and sex-appeal...

*She could dish it out, and probably outshoot any male detective...
but brother, this was one private-eye that was all woman.*

a blonde Private Eye-ful

DANGEROUS CURVES

Liz Hunter

I WAS MORE THAN a little curious as I followed the receptionist through the thickly carpeted corridor toward the office of Cy Raymond, president of Zenith Pictures. The telephone call asking me to be there had come directly from Wilbur Freeman, the head of Zenith's publicity department and a big wheel in his own right. Then as soon as I mentioned my name to the receptionist she jumped up and said, "Oh yes, Miss Hunter. Please follow me. Mr. Raymond is waiting for you."

Cy Raymond was the last of the real old-fashioned movie moguls and dictator of one of the few big film companies still flourishing. He was one of the most powerful men in the movie colony, as well as one of the shrewdest and toughest. He wouldn't be fooling with divorce scandals or paternity suits or the blackmail occasionally attempted against stars. Those were the usual reasons for movie people calling in a private investigator. But this must be something much bigger.

My curiosity increased when I followed the receptionist through the great paneled door into the huge office, and found myself the center of attention of Raymond and four of his lieutenants. They were seated at a conference table at one side of the office, which was at least 40 feet long and 25 feet wide. The room was decorated in ornate semi-Oriental modern. Raymond's big desk at the other end was ebony with glass legs, and had four white telephones on it. The rest of the place was decked out accordingly.

Raymond, a stocky little man with a heavy sun-lamp tan, wavy white hair and an arrogantly self-assured expression, looked me up and down quickly with a heavy-lidded appraising gaze that missed nothing. His thin-lipped smile was cold and calculating, but he rose and said unctuously, "It's a pleasure Miss Hunter. I'm Cy Raymond."

He nodded curtly toward a chair at his left and two of the yes men flanking him bumped into each other pulling it out from the table for me. I smiled my thanks prettily and sat down. I carefully ignored the leering glances at my knees as I crossed my legs, and calmly waited for the next move.

"THEY TOLD ME you were attractive, but I hardly expected anything so — sensational," Raymond purred. "You've got a figure, and you know how to use it." His eyes studied my legs slowly and then ex-

"I opened the bird to over a hundred miles per. The characters on my tail weren't playing footsie. I had to shake them... but fast!"

we need Liz Hunter."

"I twisted her arm behind her back, and she squealed like a stuck pig... and frankly, I couldn't see any difference"

amined the rest of me, lingering over the fitted bodice of the sheer jersey dress that clung close. "You're pretty, and furthermore you've got class. You know what? If you got half the brains they say, you're quite a girl.

"Thank you, Mr. Raymond, but I'm sure you didn't call me here for a screen test."

"No, we sure didn't," he said. "But Jeff O'Farrell appreciates feminine beauty, and this should be a help to you." His eyes narowed, and his voice took on a cold, hard edge. "Jeff O'Farrell is the hottest property in Hollywood today, and I made him. But his contract with Zenith expires after the picture he's working on now is completed. And he doesn't want to sign with us again. It's not money. We're willing to let him write his own ticket, practically. But the dumb son of a bitch has gone for a dame named Carla Montell, who's got him ready to sign with a phoney independent outfit called "Modern Productions.""

"That's not against the law," I said. "And if you just want somebody to snake him out of Carla's bed and into another, you must have a dozen sexy starlets that would do the job free."

"No, that's not our pitch," Raymond said. "This new outfit is really only a front for a bunch of the racket boys from Vegas headed by a guy named Nick Ambrazza. They don't want to produce. They'll wiggle out of that with a couple of cheap quickies and O'Farrell's percentage take'll be nothing. But what they'll do is gouge us and every other studio planning to use O'Farrell for everything we've got in so-called rent for him. They'll make a killing, but Jeff will be shafted and his box office appeal will be dead in no time. He'll lose as much as we will, but I've got to get some proof that this is so—I've got to have the goods on Carla Montell and this mob to prove it to O'Farrell, before he'll listen. It's up to you to get the proof and then 'persuade' him to listen."

This was a big one. I doubled the fee I'd planned on asking, got a healthy retainer, and set out to recapture the nation's number one male sex symbol for Zenith Productions and Elizabeth Hunter Investigations, Inc.

(Continued on page 43)

TV's PRIVATE EYES

Jacqueline Baer offers encouragement to Efrem Zimbalist Jr. as trouble shooter Louis Quinn loks on.

By FERNANDO WEST

Stu Baily and partner Jeff Spencer are bracing themselves for action in an exciting scene from "77".

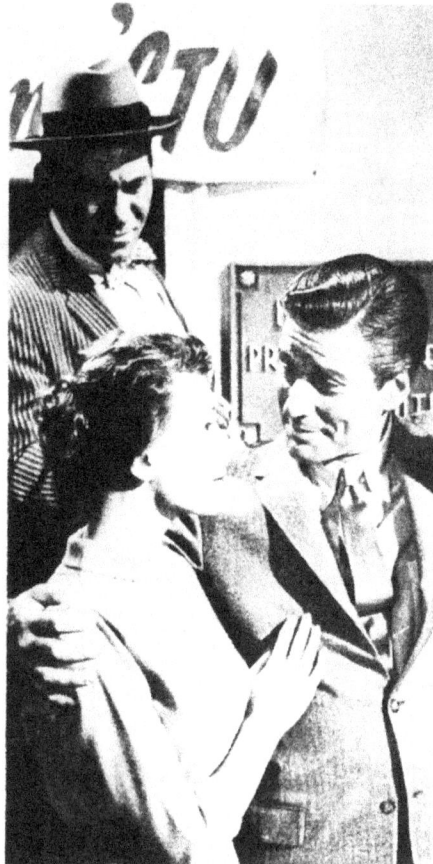

"**77 Sunset Strip**" is one of the best of the TV detective series, of the tongue-in-cheek shool. Mystery fans say they go for the stories—involved puzzlers that hold their interest till the last gunshot.

There's plenty of action: blood, bullets, blondes, redheads, and brunettes. Stuart Bailey and Jeff Spencer, the lead characters, belong to the uppercrust of the "belted trench-coaters." They make the mid-century shamus look as if he has the perfect line of work. A minimum of gumshoeing around and a lot of frosty mixed drinks at "Dino on the Strip" (Owned by Dean Martin). The plots are clever and full of twists, seem to be solved between wisecracks. The endings usually carry a **stinger** you don't expect. Backgrounds are the wide, wide world all the way from Hollywood to the Far East.

Bailey and Spencer have a classy office on the famous Hollywood "strip." Complete with a French telephone girl, Jacqueline Beer, with a built-in accent!

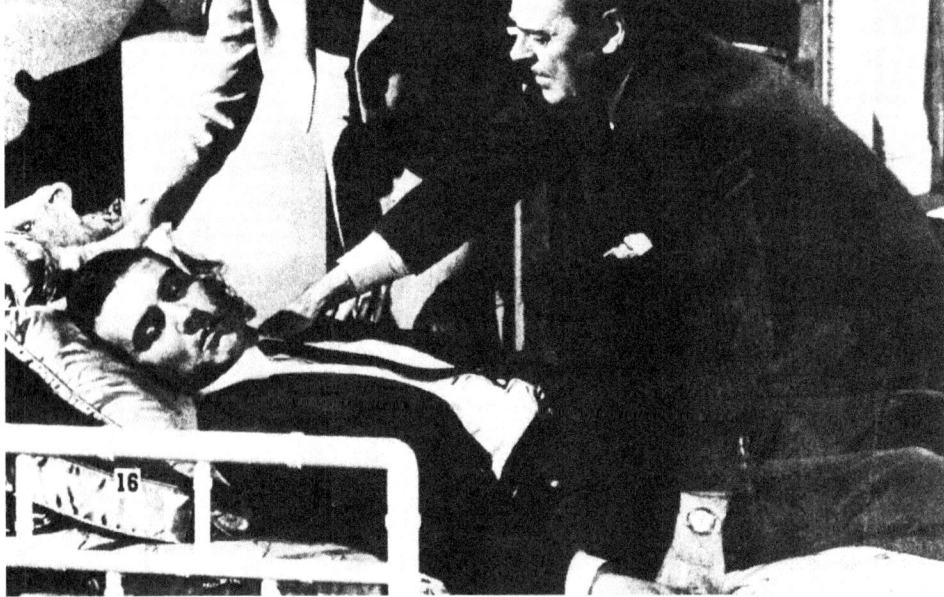

Jerome Cowan as Fenwick, trys to revive Roger Smith in the exciting "Grandma Caper" episode.

* Private Eye

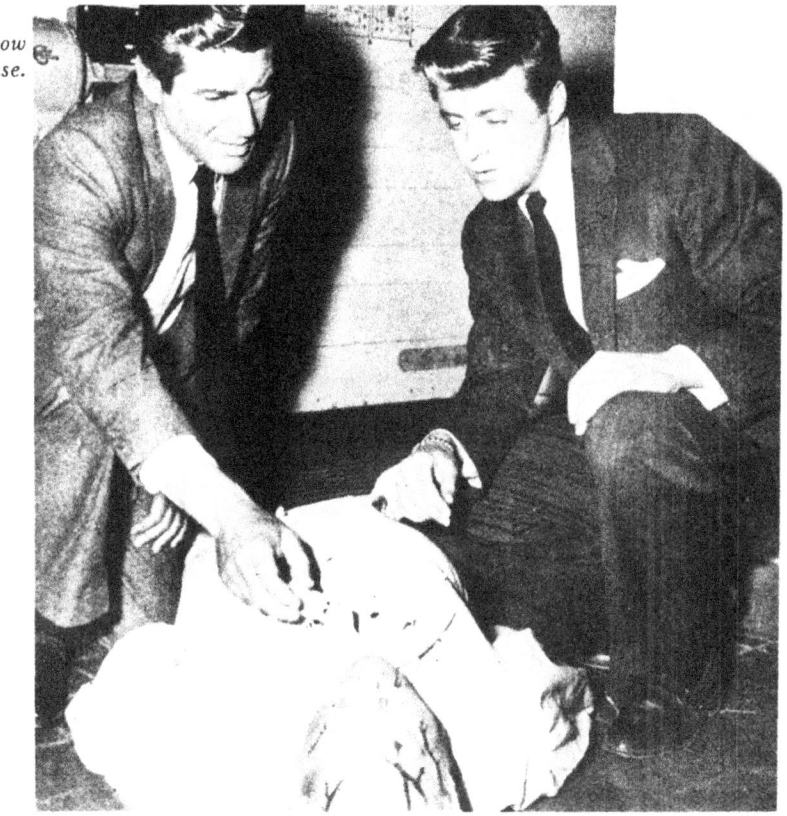

Baily gives Kookie a lesson on how to look for clues in a murder case.

A surprise of the show is "Kookie" Edd Byrnes, who plays an off-beat parking attendant. Since his success with the teen-age **screamers,** his part has been beefed up to where he joins Bailey and Spencer in their crime cases. Byrnes has good reason to cheer this series which made him a star...

"77" is one of the private shamus capers to have made it BIG. As the answer to TV westerns, they captured a large crowd of panting viewers. The brassy-but-gently manner of the two leads are in the new style of gentlemen-toughs.

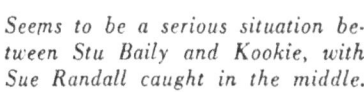

Bailey, played by suave Efrem Zimbalist, Jr., is an ex professor who has been in wartime Intelligence. With a dozen languages at his command, he plays the senior partner. Roger Smith as Jeff Spencer is the junior exec and boyish, not as polished as his sidekick, but just as **brainy.**

Solving crimes isn't the only thing Kookie has learned from the two masters. Girl is the beautiful Laurie Mitchell.

Seems to be a serious situation between Stu Baily and Kookie, with Sue Randall caught in the middle.

TV's PRIVATE EYES

Some shows have been .. "Hit and Run." In this one, Kookie has the grief—an old time star claims she has been disfigured in an auto crash with Kookie. Operative Bailey comes to the rescue, with evidence that clears him.

"Lovely Alibi"— Ed, a policeman friend of Bailey's, is suspended because he accuses an influencial man of murder. The suspect is pinned down after Ed's girlfriend is mysteriously threatened. Spencer steps in again.

"Hong Kong Caper."— A letter to a wealthy man sends Jeff Spencer to China. This starts off a strange yarn in which Oriental characters threaten his life. All ends well—and in time for the last commercial...

"Casualty"— is a story where a **dead man** seems to be very much alive. With Kookie helping to solve the puzzle, Spencer uncovers a nest of gangsters.

Looks as if Jeff Spencer is in real serious trouble.

But only for a moment as Private Eye Spencer quickly turns the tables.

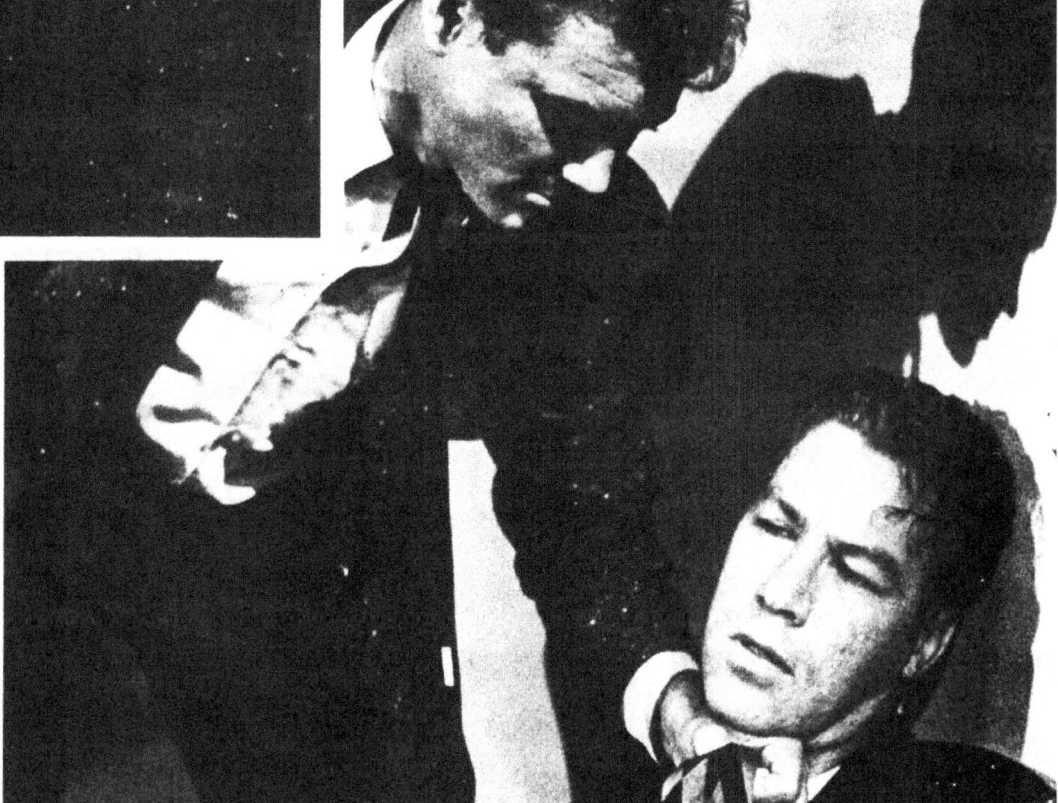

18 * Private Eye

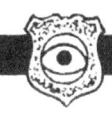  Private Eye

Kookie offers encouragement to Jeff Spencer and his very pretty client.

A dash of comedy is added by Roscoe, a bookie who is a pal of the two dicks. Roscoe has underworld connections but he's a good egg—never steals from friends!

ABC considers this show one of its best and it looks like it will be around a long, long time. To its off trail stories, "77" keeps adding interesting characters and keeps hitting the target.

✶ ✶ ✶

Jeff Spencer prepares to fire his tear-gas gun. There's always excitement and action in ABC TV's "77 SUNSET STRIP."

We can't blame Stu for concentrating on his very pretty client.

Mark Randall hadn't heard that voice in ten years. But it was a call to arms he couldn't refuse. Mystery, intrigue and excitement lie ahead, and the beautiful readheaded Irene Tedescu was at the end of the line.

RED means BLOOD

by GARY STEVENS

THE LIGHT SNAPPED GREEN and Mark Randall revved the gold tone T-Bird over the garage ramp and into the thin stream of post-mid-night traffic along New York's Fifth Avenue. He nosed the car south past the fountains in the Plaza and the dimly lit Rococco hotels. As the blacktop roadway rolled away under the two-seater, Randall's mind was racing as fast as the eager engine.

Fifteen minutes ago he was Mark Randall, professionally respected and socially prominent bachelor lawyer sitting in the ease of his east side duplex apartment. Then the phone rang and in a few hurried words ten years of his life were washed away.

Mark thought back to the early years just after the war when his Army counter-intelligence job landed him in Berlin where he played a dangerous game of tag with ruthless Soviet agents. Now it was to begin all over again.

When the phone rang in his library, Randall lazily put down the legal brief he was reading and stretched his six-foot, well muscled frame over to the desk and picked up the ringing telephone.

"Hello," he said, thinking perhaps it was a friend, or at worst some anxious client with a problem that couldn't wait until morning. The voice on the other end belonged to no client and certainly wasn't mellow enough to be one of Randall's sophisticated lady friends.

"Hello Randall?"

"Yes," he answered.

"This is Nick Warden..."

"Nick!" interrupted Randall...

The voice on the other end said, "No questions. Just listen. Meet me in the snack bar of the ferry that leaves for Staten Island at twenty minutes after midnight. Will you do it?"

Without a second thought Randall listened to the voice of the man who had been his boss in postwar Germany and said, "Yes, I'll be there."

He heard the click as the line went dead on the other end.

Randall shucked out of his raw silk dressing gown and reached under the desk to a hidden drawer. He drew out an English Webley .38 cal. in a shining black shoulder holster and eased into the harness, buckling it on as he moved towards the hall closet. His mind was already going.

It had been almost ten years since he had last heard from Nick Warden, then a Colonel and now a Brigadier General, and he knew that the meeting tonight was going to be something more than a social call. *(Continued on page 46)*

Randall smashed his way inside, and even in the exchange of heated gunfire he could not help noticing the voluptuous Irene Tedescu.

Ina Gardner on this page, and Martha Howell on the next page can make things pretty exciting for any virile Private-Eye. As far as we're concerned, they're both our...

FAVORITE SUSPECT

Ina Gardner
Suspect No. 1

Sherlock Holmes never had it so good.

Martha Howell
Suspect No. 2

Here's a perfect shot for your rogues gallery.

The PUBLIC'S PRIVATE EYE

F. B. I. Chief Hoover called them, "The most vicious, dangerous and resourceful criminal brains this country ever produced."

THE BARKER-KARPIS GANG

by LEON LAZARUS

"COME OUT WITH YOUR HANDS UP and you won't get hurt." The words boomed loudly in the misty, pre-dawn light, then died away. The silence returned. Nothing stirred. The cottage, shaded by Royal Palms, betrayed no movement. Overhead, the last star faded from view.

His jacket collar turned up against the chilling mist, Walter Ferris, an F.B.I. special investigator, turned to his fellow agent beside him.

"I'm going to make one more try," he whispered. "If that doesn't work—" He paused. "Well, then you know what to do, Dave."

Dave McMorris, one of the department's crack shots, carefully slipped his machine-gun off safety.

"Right," he whispered. "Only you be careful."

Ferris nodded grimly, then slipped forward toward the house. Some twenty yards off he stopped and once again cupped his hands to his mouth. "This is your last chance," he cried. "If you don't come out we'll use tear gas and force you out."

An ominous pause followed, then all hell broke loose. Bursts of orange flame blazed from an upper window and the air was shattered by the smash and whine of machine-gun fire. A burst of bullets tore up the ground at Ferris' feet. A second burst whipped overhead. A third volley thudded at his heels as he leaped for cover.

Now the battle was on in earnest as the F.B.I. men returned the fire, only their job wasn't going to be easy. They were up against a pair of desperate criminals. *J. Edgar Hoover*, director of the *Federal Bureau of Investigation*,

(Continued on page 26)

Karpis opened fire. Within seconds the police were returning the fire.

THE BARKER-KARPIS GANG

called them; "the most vicious, dangerous and resourceful criminal brains this country has ever produced."

Oddly enough, one of them was a woman, the notorious *Ma Barker*. The other was Fred Barker, her youngest and favorite son. Their blood-splotched careers had its beginning many years before. For a full decade the sinister Barker-Karpis Gang had preyed upon a law abiding society. Their activities ranged from bank robery and kidnaping to *murder!*

BEHIND ALL OF THE GANG'S operations was the evil genius of Ma Barker. Born in the Ozarks near Ashgrove, Missouri, she married one George E. Barker in 1892 and in time bore him four sons. There was Herman, Lloyd, Arthur and the aforesaid Fred. By the time they were in their teens all of her sons had been in trouble with the law. What "*steamed*" Ma wasn't the fact that her children had broken the law, but that they had allowed themselves to be *caught!*

When her oldest son, Herman, was picked up in Webb City, Mo., on a theft charge, she admonished him with a piece of advice that she would repeat over and over through the years.

"Don't answer questions," she snapped. "Remember. Say nothing, lose *nothing!*"

The boys took this advice to heart, and when the Barkers moved to Tulsa, Oklahoma, they had it down pat. Here they joined up with a group known as the *Central Park Gang*. It was petty thievery mostly, a kind of "prep" schooling for the criminal careers they were destined to follow.

In time, the Barker household became a kind of headquarters with Ma in command. Young thugs and hoodlums came to her with their problems and Ma supplied the answers. She sharpened their methods, improved their techniques. In short, because of her counseling they became more cunning, more ruthless. Before long her reputation spread through the underworld and more and more of her sons' gangster friends frequented her place. It was out of these gatherings that the Barker Gang began to emerge.

Ma Barker and her favorite son, Fred, remain inseparable in death as in life.

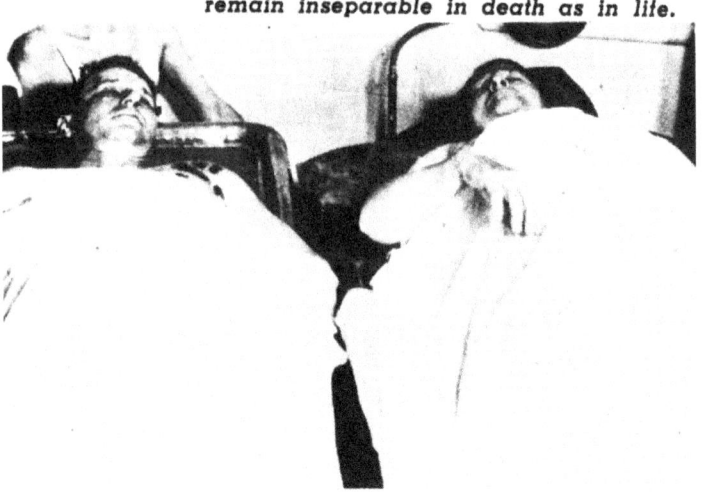

BY THE TIME THE ROARING TWENTIES broke upon the American scene, the Baxter Gang was a flourishing institution. Operating under Ma's instructions the youthful killers and gunmen cut a bloody swath throughout the mid-west. For her supervisory skills Ma took a good cut, but no one complained. Everyone was in the chips. Everyone was doing great.

In their various hideouts wild parties were staked between their sorties in crime. Illegal whiskey and girls were plentiful. On one occasion, as the girls cut up, Ma flipped. Some of the molls had kicked off their shoes and wriggled out of their tight skirts. One of them was doing a strip tease on a table and was down to her panties. The boys were howling and cheering her on.

"That's enough," Ma shrieked when she burst in on the scene.

She dragged the girl off the table and slapped her across the face. "Put your clothes on and clear out," she demanded. She faced the other girls. "And that goes for the pack of you."

The girls didn't argue. Her temper up, Ma was a tigress. Silently they picked their clothes off the floor and filed out.

"Gee, Ma," Freddy protested, "Why'd you break it up just when it was getting interesting?"

Ma grunted. "Interesting nothing. If I let you kids have things your own way you'd be finished outside of a month. Liquor and women have their place, but up to a point. You boys went way past it."

AS THE TWENTIES DREW ON, however, the Barker "luck" came to a temporary halt. Arthur was serving a life term in Oklahoma State Prison for the murder of a watchman. Lloyd was in Leavenworth for robbing the U. S. mail. Fred was in Kansas State Penitentiary for larceny.

The only one out was Herman, but fate had its own plans for Ma's oldest. He and a gunman by the name of Ray Terril had teamed up, with Ma as usual in charge of the strategy. Time and again they knocked off banks in Kansas and Missouri. Chased but not caught, they fought many a gun battle with pursuing police. Then, in 1927, after holding up an ice-station, they were stopped and questioned by J. E. Marshall, a traffic officer. As the policeman prodded them with questions, the trigger nervous Herman whiped out his gun and came up shooting. In the brief battle the policeman dropped to the ground mortally wounded. Herman and Terrill fled.

Witnesses positively identified Herman as the killer and the search was on. It ended however, with the discovery of Herman's body in a patch of weeds outside of Wichita. His death was listed as a suicide, but the bullet wound may not have been self-inflicted. It is altogether probable that the bullet came from the policeman's gun.

With Herman dead and the other boys in jail, the Barker Gang was momentarily out of business. For Ma it was disquieting hiatus. During this period her husband, who was thoroughly fed up with his family's criminal career, packed up and left. He wasn't missed. Ma took up with a younger man, a gunman by the name of Arthur Dunlop.

For awhile things poked along and then Fred, Ma's favorite, was released from the Kansas penitentiary. While in jail, however, Fred had made the acquaintance of a gunman by the name of Alvin Karpis. Out of this friendship an unholy alliance was to be formed—a merging of criminal "talents" unequalled in the annals of crime.

FOLLOWING FRED'S RELEASE, Karpis soon regained his freedom, only without benefit of parole or pardon. While in solitary confinement for infraction of prison rules, Karpis somehow got his hands on a saw and hacked his way out. Fleeing to Chicago he joined the

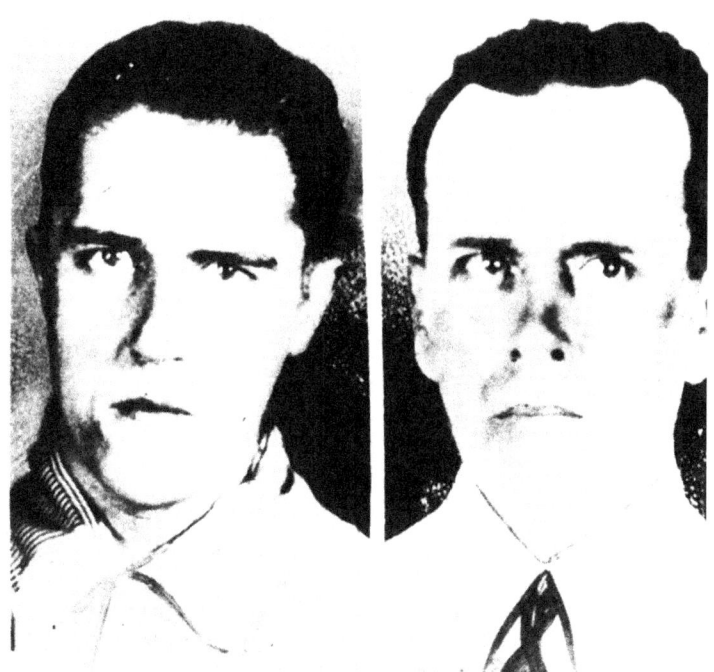

Alvin Karpis, left, and Arthur Barker, right, were credited as two of the criminal brains behind the kidnapping of Edward G. Bremer.

The door crashed open, and in seconds all hell was breaking loose.

Barkers and operations for the country's biggest crime spree was in the making.

By 1931, after holding up an exclusive shop in Missouri, Karpis and Fred rode the getaway car into a garage for repairs. A gun duel with a pursuing sheriff followed and the law officer was slain by the two killers. This prompted the gang to flee and St. Paul became their new base of operations.

Ma was furious at the start. "You've got no brains," she wailed. "You never should've taken that car to a garage. Killing that sheriff was pretty stupid."

"Maybe." Fred sulked, "only it was either him or us."

In St. Paul the gang went into high gear. Bank robberies became their specialty. Ma did the planning, in many cases picking banks as far distant as 200 miles from the hideout. Every detail was carefully checked, and before departing, like a military operation, Ma would give her boys their final briefing.

"Now remember," she'd caution them. "In this place you'll do better with machine-guns. Flash them the minute you get inside. The place ain't too big and you'll be able to cover everyone easy. Now get going, and don't anyone slip up—or else!"

Many of these bank robberies came off without a flaw. On other occasions the unexpected might happen. A teller would sound a secret alarm and the fireworks would begin. Ruthlessly the gang would cut down anyone who got in their way. With a kind of sadistic glee they'd sweep the area with machine-gun fire as they'd back toward the getaway car. Then off in a burst of speed, the crumpled bodies of their innocent victims sprawled amidst the smoldering ruins.

DURING THIS PERIOD, as the notorious gunmen plundered and killed, their activities were not unknown to the F. B. I. Every deed of violence they committed was duly noted. Still, the G-men were unable to act. The Barker-Karpis Gang hadn't as yet violated a federal law. Until such time their apprehension was the responsibility of state and local police.

Meanwhile, under Ma's strategy, the gang shifted around from St. Paul to Reno, Kansas City, Chicago and back to St. Paul. Then, in 1932, Arthur Barker was released from the Oklahoma prison and when he rejoined the gang a new act had been added to their criminal repertoire. Kidnapping had come into "vogue" and it didn't take Ma long to con the gang into giving it a whirl.

Their first victim was William A. Hamm, Jr., a wealthy St. Paul brewer. Four days later, after payment of $100,000 in ransom money, Hamm was released.

The gang kicked up their heels. They took up luxurious quarters in Chicago's South Shore Drive and wild parties

(Continued on page 52)

WHO WILL BE *Miss Private Eye?*

Here are some of our selections for this issue's Miss Private-Eye. Why not send in photos of your favorite nomination. Those selected will appear on this page every issue. Send photos to... Miss Private-Eye, c/o Calyork Features, Inc., 24 West 45th St., New York 36, N. Y.

Georgia Bell
Atlanta, Ga.

Helene Smith
Dallas, Tex.

Valerie Jordan
Brooklyn, N. Y.

Even cops and robbers has its lighter side as we found out when we asked cartoonists Bill Riley and Don Oreheck to do up a few entitled...

THIS IS A LAUGH-UP

"Let's face it Miriam—you're spending it faster than I can make it."

"I don't want to leave any fingerprints!"

"I SMASHED THE VICE-PHOTO RACKET"

By TOM NOLAN

They say one picture is worth a thousand words. Only in this case it was more than one picture, and worth a hell of a lot more than one thousand words. And my life was at stake...

THE GIRL DANCED NAKED with her breasts bouncing like air inflated balloons while the man grabbed her by the arm and pulled her down onto the mussed up bed.

Out in the audience men whistled and laughed and clapped their hands. Then the police burst through the doorway and a raid was in progress.

I learned about it only an hour later when my former boss, Captain of Detectives Pat Monohan, phoned me at the agency office. In a confidential voice, he said, "Tom, if you've got nothing else to do for the next hour, stop by the shop."

I had nothing else to do. The other two members of my three man Acme Investigations, Inc., were out on the routine security lift prowl and an insurance claim investigation. So I went down the street to Pat's office.

The station house was heavy with familiarity, for I'd worked out of here as a Lieutenant on the 11th Detective Squad for six years until I'd turned in my tin for the right to be my own boss. That had been three years ago and I'd prospered since then well as a small agency can.

So I went through the duty sergeant's room and winked at the white haired old man in uniform who would sit there until the day he retired. I went right on back without challenge. Monohan's office was in the rear.

Private Eye

Some of the girls were real dolls

Two men were present when I entered. One of them was white haired, with a big, rawboned face and shreds of tobacco clinging to his mouth where he chewed his cigars apart. That was Pat Monohan, a lifetime cop who had been my boss. In a way I suppose he still thought of me as one of his boys. That was why he tossed business my way. This time he was tossing me the portly, balding, jowl heavy man in the undertaker's shiny black suit.

"This is Mr. Chewett," the captain said. Then he added, pointing to me. "And this is Tom Nolan, the peeper I told you about. He once worked for me and now he's his own boss. I don't know if either one is a recommendation. But he'll give you an honest day's labor and he won't steal your money and that's the most I guess you can expect from any man."

The name, Chewett, was familiar but I didn't place it until Monohan went on, this time speaking to me. "Mr. Chewett here is a chairman of the Committee Against Obscenity. It's a private group that battles immoral practices in town. He's a little unhappy with the Department's Vice Squad at the moment. Mr. Chewett thinks they're not doing enough to wipe out the spread of pornographic literature and films that seem to be flooding in." The Captain hesitated a moment, then added dryly. "Can't say that I blame him. I'm

(Continued on next page)

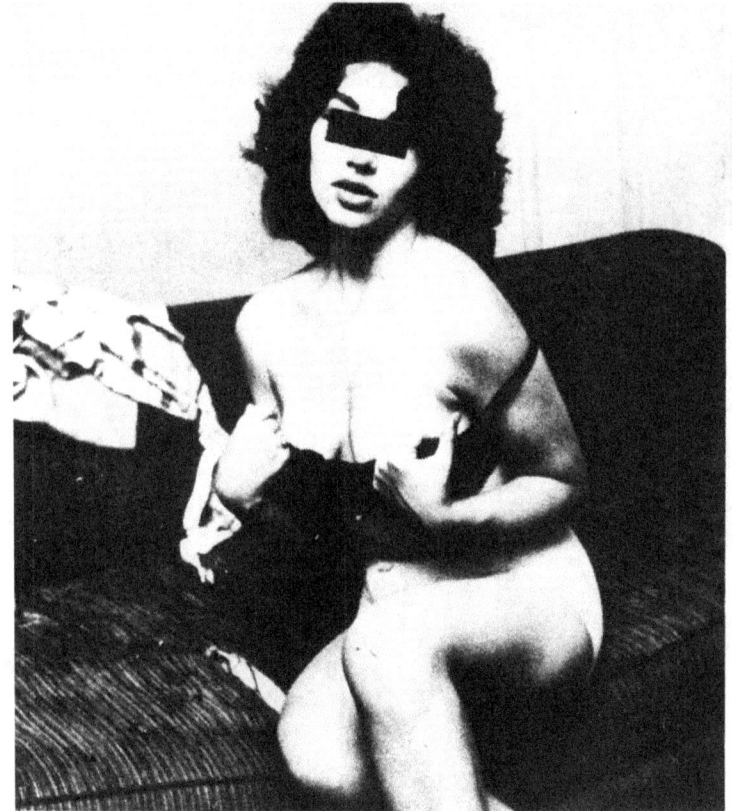

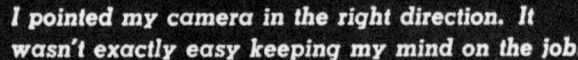

I pointed my camera in the right direction. It wasn't exactly easy keeping my mind on the job.

"I SMASHED THE VICE-PHOTO RACKET"

not satisfied either. But then the syndicate that's spreading this scum seems to have most of our Department boys pegged. We haven't been able to get a man inside... so, when Mr. Chewett suggested a private investigator, I came up with your name." Monohan's smile had a frosted edge but it was the most warmth he ever showed. "I figured you could use the money..."

I KNEW THE RACKET he was referring to. In fact, in an occasional piece of divorce business I used a couple of the well dimensioned hookers who picked up easy money posing for indecent pictures. It wouldn't be a tough assignment for me. But I didn't want word around the Department that I was claiming to be able to do a job they couldn't handle. So I played it modest. "That's all right, Captain. I'm glad to help. But why should Mr. Chewett be upset. Some of the Vice Squad boys did raid a stag party about an hour ago where they had the picture setup rigged...

For the first time Chewett spoke. Although his lips were pursed there was a suggestion of a twinkle in his eye. "Yes..." he said. "Only they thought it was a teen-age dance and made the raid to get some of the kids for curfew violation..."

Even Monohan had trouble hiding his grin on that one. And I held out my hand. "Mr. Chewett, you've just hired yourself an operator." When he grasped mine in return I was surprised. There was a strong grip in those flabby looking fingers.

First thing I did was get a look at the mob they picked up in the raid on the stag party an hour before. The cops were still processing them through a magistrate's office where they were given a slap on the wrist and told to go and sin no more. There were about four hundred slobs picked up and only two hundred of them had gone through the mill. I spotted my guy immediately. He was probably the most innocent looking one of the lot; a meek little fellow with deep sunk eyes and a tic along the left side of his mouth. His name was Bruno Kluve. Though he was a photographer by profession, he made his money by distributing pornographic literature and acting as doorman and general helper at obscene demonstrations. At these last events, slobs, for a fee averaging twenty five to fifty bucks a head, could come, get a camera, and either take pictures to their heart's content or just stand there with their tongues hanging out and the drool running down their vests.

I let a cellblock screw know that Bruno and I had to have words in private. The turnkey started to give me an argument until I told him to check Monohan. A minute later he was back from the phone and I got a private alcove in one corner. Only for us. Bruno and I.

(Continued on page 60)

She certainly knew her stuff. It wasn't the first time she's had her picture taken.

YOU BE A PRIVATE EYE

THE CARR CASE MYSTERY

On the evening of March 22nd, 1952, detective Martin Paine was called to Pine Lodge. Waiting at the door was frightened Mr. Bailey.

Trembling with emotion, Bailey led the detective into the dimly lit study. From an overhead beam hung a lifeless body.

The dead man was Dave Carr, Bailey's business partner. They were spending the weekend alone at their country place.

As detective Paine looked things over, Bailey continued. His partner wasn't a well man. He had been despondent. Spoke of suicide.

The police were notified. On examining the body, detective Paine found positive rope burns on the dead man's neck.

Calling the dead man's doctor in the city, Bailey's statement was confirmed. Carr wasn't well, and he brooded a great deal.

The coroner's report summed it up. Death was due to asphyxiation by hanging. It appeared as a very clear cut case of suicide.

But then came the shocking surprise. Detective Martin Paine disagreed! Carr hadn't died by his own hand. He had been murdered.

Turning suddenly toward Bailey, detective Paine pointed an accusing finger. "And here is his murderer," he announced.

solution on page 44

Girl Friday to a PRIVATE

The hours are rotten... The pay is looow... the working conditions are brutal. But MM (Monica March) is crazy about her job as No. 1 girl to a Private Shamus.

The day starts with her boss giving dictation. Knowing how to take shorthand is not very important.

Some unexpected company, but Monica's in top shape.

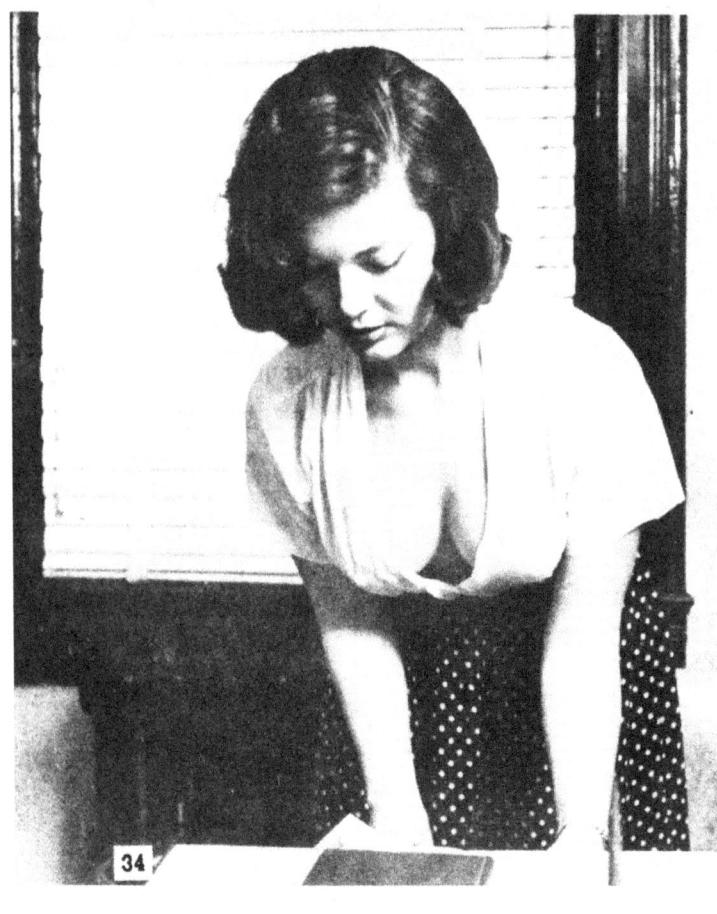

On the job-training includes casing the joint for hidden narcotics, blackmail letters, and a dime for a cup of coffee.

* Private Eye

Phoning for the coppers gives her a chance to sit down. It's getting to be a rough day.

EYE

In this business, A girl can't be to careful.

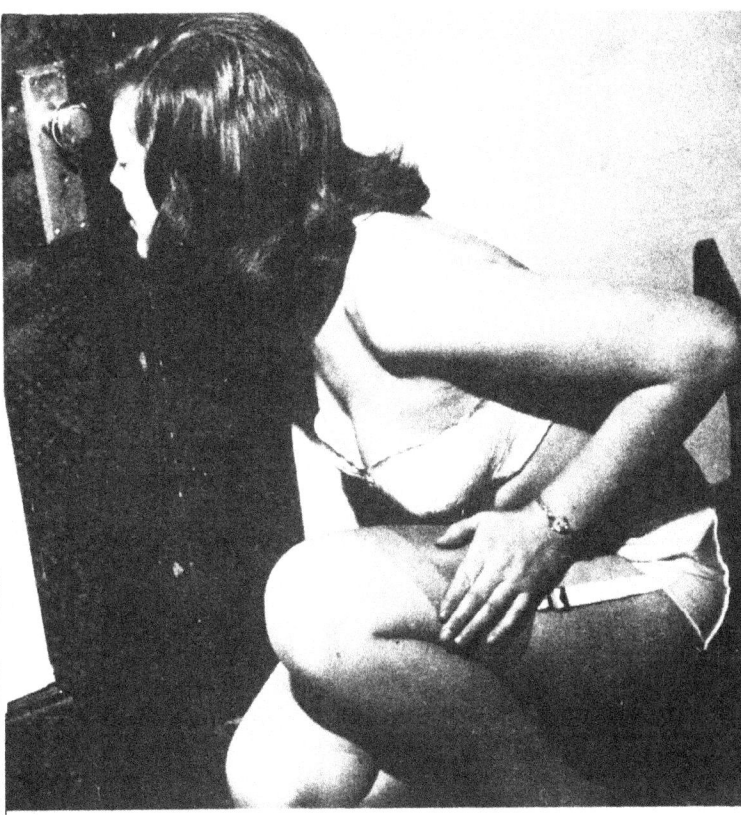

Studying fingerprints can be very important. But while Monica studies her fingerprints, we'll study Monica.

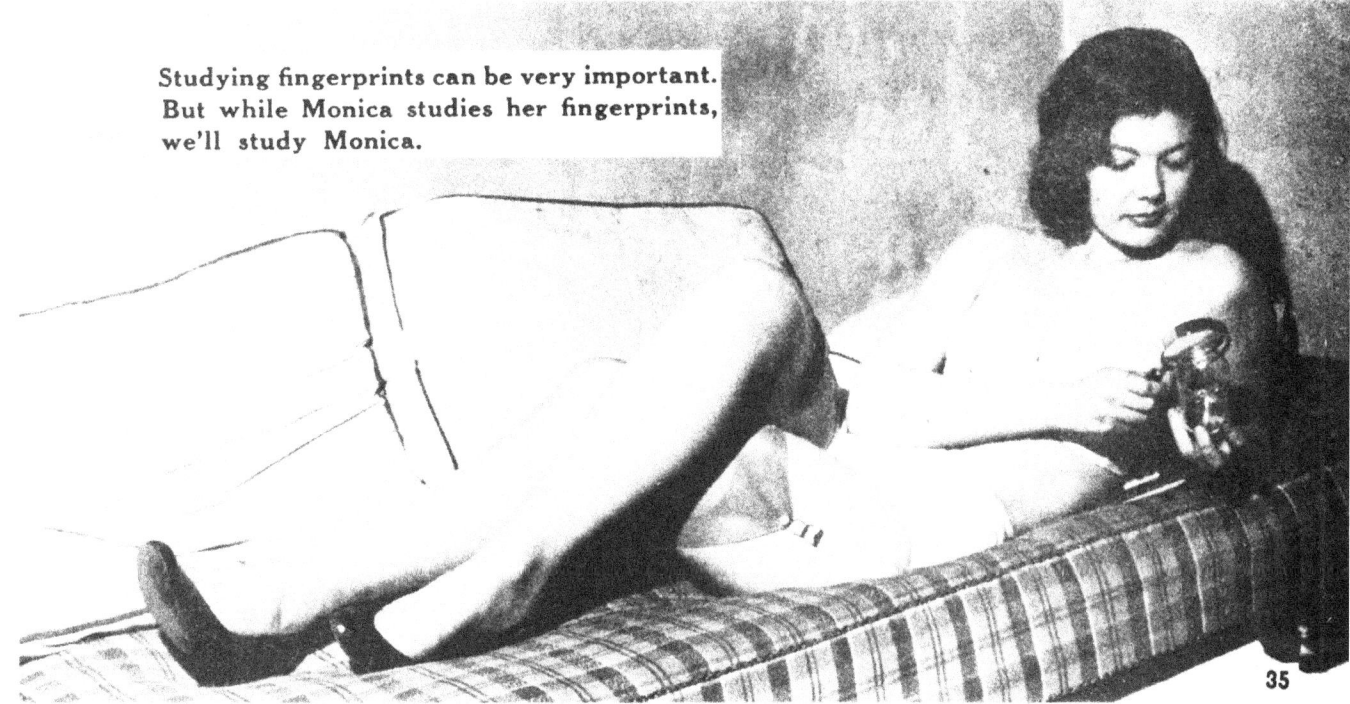

"I felt a whistle past my ear, and a chunk of building flew past my nose. My own gun was spitting return lead as I threw both girls to the side."

SAM MENNING PRIVATE EYE

IN

BOSOMS

Greenwich Village can be pretty exciting. But it sure went wild when I took on two cute South American packages as my clients.

I KEPT TRYING TO SHAKE the cobwebs out of my head. Man, did I get a going over last night. The divorce case I was working on for weeks finally came to a head when I caught the evidence and the big tank of a guy she was with in the parked car. Only for a private-eye, I forgot my lessons and edged too close. This big hulk spotted me, and used my head for a punching bag. The beard I had grown years before was no protection, and I could swear he grabbed me by it and threw me for a touchdown.

My mind was made up. At least the part that could think. As soon as I could get to my feet, I was going to tell that client of mine to go to hell. I'd send him his retainer back and let him get himself another bird. Besides, he was playing around plenty. I'm no judge, but I'd call this case a draw.

The phone ringing in my Greenwich Village apartment office snapped me out of my thoughts. In fact, at this point it sounded like a squad of fire engines, all in my room, with the sirens going at full blast.

FOR A SECOND, I figured I was in heaven. This was the sexiest voice I ever heard. I'm certainly no Gable,

and BULLETS

but I sure felt like it right now. "Hello, Mr. Menning?" Mr. Menning yet. I haven't been called formally for so long now, that I almost forgot it was my last name. "Yes, this is him..." I could feel no more pain. "Mr. Menning, I wonder if you would be good enough to take my case. That is, my sister and myself would like to retain you for a few days." Now that she spoke a little longer, I could detect an accent. Man, I could just visualize the face behind the voice. It was the ginchiest. "Tell me a few of the facts honey, like your name and what you have in mind." I knew what *I* had in mind. "My name is Violeta Juarez, and my sister's name is Maria. I can't tell you any more over the phone." "Okay, c'mon up to my place. Do you have the address?" A few seconds of silence and then, "No, it would be best if you could meet us at the Dew Drop Inn on East Eighth St. We are there now. Please do not disappoint us Mr. Menning, we are in dire need of your services." It was real crazy, but I was beginning to smell perfume over the phone. That beating I took really affected me. "Be right there Violet." How could I resist the perfume? I took a shower and got dressed. As a matter of fact, I was tempted to shave my beard. But I couldn't go that far. The beard was my identification, and my passport to the beatnik crowd. They understood me and I understood them. No, I couldn't go that far.

I felt better as soon as I hit the air. The beret tilted on my head, and thoughts of two beautiful clients instilled an air of confidence in me. The Dew Drop Inn was a short walk from my place. I knew it well, as I did everything else in the Village. This was my town, my village. This was the area I chose to work from five years ago when I became an official Private-eye. After all, I had it all figured out at the time. I certainly was no T. V. detective. Five ten and a hundred fifty pounds didn't make me eligible to take on cases that involved slugging it out hand to hand with the kind of hoods they showed on the screen. No sir, I stuck strictly to routine stuff and divorce cases. Only after the case I came up against last night, I was seriously thinking of knocking that off my list as too damned dangerous. I packed a rod, but I've never considered trying to use it even as a threat. I was entitled to carry one so I did. However, I made it my business to go down to the gun club once a month and practice marksmanship. Of that I was proud. There wasn't anything over a thirty-secondth of an inch that I couldn't hit. *(Continued on next page)*

37

BOSOMS and BULLETS

THE DEW DROP INN was just that. The first step down was so steep that if you weren't conscious of it, you could land on your noggin'. Maybe it wasn't a bad idea at that. The gootch they served you inside was so bad, it paid to go in a little groggy. I wondered why Violet picked this spot to meet.

"Mr. Menning, I presume?" My head turned to follow the scent of a heavenly aroma. In fact, I thought my head would never stop turning. Two of them. Two of the most gorgeous dark haired *señoritas* I have ever seen. And stacked to the gils. "Miss Juarez? But how did you know it was me?" "Surely you are joking, no? Your beard Mr. Manning." I tried to pass it off as a joke, but I sure felt foolish inside. I decided enough was enough. Grow up Sam, find out what this is all about and take it or leave it. I sat down at their table. It was barely two in the afternoon, and the place was empty except for the sloppy looking bartender putting on the ball game.

"O. K. girls, let's have it. What's the bit? Give."

"Mr. Menning, the reason we wish to retain you is that they think we saw a murder committed." This was the first time Maria spoke, and since she didn't make much sense, I directed myself to Violet. "Suppose you give it to me again honey, only this time in American. And forgosh sakes, call me Sam. You gals are giving me a complex with that Mr. Menning stuff." Violet picked up her cue. "Sam, we are models from Ponta-Diago, a small country in South America. We are here to model some of our fashions for your how you say it, high society? Last night at one of these functions, Maria and I walked into the garden to get some air after we have modeled. We heard two men arguing violently. We didn't stay, but as we walked back in, we met one of the men. He didn't say anything to us, but when we got back to our hotel room a few hours later the phone rang, and it was him. He told us to keep our mouths shut about the man that was murdered, or my sister and I would get it. Then he changed his mind and said we would get it anyway. Sam, we're afraid. Only this morning as we left the hotel, we saw two hard looking men lurking outside. That's why we called you from here."

This was *great*. If I helped the girls out, I was breaking my rule of handling dangerous cases. This could mean real trouble. Peter Gunn would take it in a minute, and wrap it up within three commercials. But as for me, it was a different story. I'd have to think it over. Figure out my fee. I looked at Maria, and then I looked at Violet. I took another deep breath and caught a whiff of that sexy perfume they both used... I took the case.

AFTER TALKING TO THEM some more, I found out that they would be modeling at one other very high-class shindig tomorrow night, and the morning after they would be taking a plane back to their own country. They found my number in the phone book and since I was close to the Dew Drop Inn they called me. I pointed out that my beard and beret was a dead give-away, and they pointed out that they *wanted* it known I was protecting them. It might discourage any further threats and possibly scare off the hoods until the girls are safely out of the country.

It started to rain as we climbed into the cab. "Hotel Eastwood driver."

On the way up to the fourteenth floor, I asked some more questions. "To tell you the truth girls, I haven't seen a paper or listened to a radio since yesterday afternoon. What did the press have to say about the murder?" "Sam, that's the funny thing about it, nobody said a word. It wasn't in any of the papers. Maria and I thought about going to the police, but what can we tell them. Somebody saw a murder? What murder? It all sounds so foolish."

Violet was right, of course, and I was going to suggest the cops, but first I wanted to know some more. "Look honey, you don't happen to know the guy's name that called you by any chance?" "No Sam, I never saw him before last night." "One more thing, where did this society show take place, and who gave it?" The elevator stopped, and we walked down the corridor. "It was given by Mrs. William Wentworth, of Long Island. I don't know the exact address, we were escorted there. Everything, our whole tour was arranged in advance."

Maria put the key in the door, and I walked in first. I put my hand on the light switch, and as it went on I caught a glimpse of one of the biggest fists I've ever seen... and it caught me right on the left eye. I didn't see the other hand, but I sure felt it... right in the gut. I could feel my head bouncing against the wall as I slowly sagged towards the floor, and I also knew I was taking a few kicks in the belly for good measure. Then everything went black.

SLOWLY THE COBWEBS began to clear. Out of the foggy foggy dew, I saw the most beautiful bosoms I have ever seen. They were covered by a sheer negligee, and when the picture became clearer I was able to make out Violet. "Sam, Sam, you poor boy. Drink some of this water." I started to pick my head up and the room began to spin. Little Sam stay-out-of-trouble sure picked a lulu this time. The divorce case was beginning to look tame compared to this. "O. K., whose husband hit me? Or is this a sample of how to get a revolution started." Violet managed to shut me up by pouring some water down my throat. I could see Maria also in a negligee sitting on the couch. Boy if this was a joint, two babes like this didn't have to go to all that trouble to get customers. Hell, I could've brought friends by the carload.

"It was two men, Sam. The same two that we saw earlier in the day."

Violet pitched in. "As soon as those brutes attacked you Sam, we started to scream our lungs out, people came out from all the rooms and that scared the men away." I put my hands to my swollen face. It probably looked like a Picasso by now.

"Sam, get some sleep. We have a big day and night ahead of us. I don't think they'll bother us again tonight."

I spent the next day watching the girls try on clothes they were to fashion that night at the swank hotel apartment of wealthy dowager Hanna Van

(Continued on page 45)

MESSAGE OF MURDER

I WAS ON MY WAY OUT when the phone rang. I snapped a cigarette from my pack, lit up and waited. The phone kept going. By the sixth ring I knew it was no use. I kicked the door shut with my heel and crossed back to the desk. I snatched it up, halfway through the next ring, waited a second, then gave it my professional, solid-citizen tone.

"Adam Baxter speaking."

There was this silence, and for a second I thought the line had gone dead. Suddenly a man's voice broke through. "Baxter," it rasped, "this is Peter J. Warren."

The name didn't ring a bell, but there was a peculiar hollow tone to the voice, as though he were speaking down a pipe. There was another pause, so I waited.

Suddenly it was back. "You still there, Baxter?"

I made a grunting sound.

"What's your business?" he growled. I let the smoke out slowly. I said: "I've got an appointment with Mr. Warren."

"I've got to see you," it went on. "You've been highly recommended."

"By whom?"

He brushed past it. "You've got to come up today. This afternoon."

I glanced up at the wall clock over the file. The little hand was on the three and the big hand was nudging it. I was thinking of a hot shower and the cozy dinner Carol had planned at her place. It was a very tempting thought.

"Look," I said, "it's Saturday afternoon, there's another client I have to see, so how about buzzing me on Monday morning, Mr. Warren. It can hold, can't it?"

"It can't," he snapped. "Someone's out to *kill* me!"

BY TEN AFTER THREE I was fighting the traffic north along the West Side Highway.

I edged my Pontiac through the bronze gates of Warren's estate at a little past four.

It looked very slick and very expensive.

It was a big stucco job, very elegant, but not to my taste.

There were a few tables beside the patio and a sprinkling of lounging chairs. There were also two county police cars with their big silver stars painted on the doors.

I hit the brakes and cut the ignition. I had just lit my cigarette when a big, freckled-faced trooper pushed his head through the open side window.

"What's your business?" he growled.

I let the smoke out slowly. I said: "I've got an appointment with Mr. Warren."

He gave me his shrewd look—the corny bit with the eyelids squeezed down to thin slits. "What about?"

I shrugged. "Let's find Mr. Warren and we'll both learn something."

He stiffened and yanked open the door. "*Out!*" he barked.

I wasn't going to argue, but I didn't break any records getting out. It was a real nasty silence and then there was the crunch of footsteps from behind.

We both turned.

There were three of them. The girl was a slender shapely blonde, on the tall side and looked spoiled. The young man could have been her brother. He was younger, not much over twenty. The stocky man in the rumpled, grey suit had policeman written all over him. It happened I was right on all three counts.

THE STOCKY GUY turned out to be Detective Boyle. He wasn't volunteering information, and when he put the questions to me I didn't hedge. Boyle was no amateur fresh out of police training school. He was a seasoned, slick pro. I told him about Warren calling me, wanting to see me, but I left out the bit about Warren's nervousness—his feeling that someone was out to kill him.

"Then you don't know why he wanted to see you?" he prodded.

"Other than it was important—no."

I gave him my big, dumb look. "Anything wrong with Mr. Warren?"

"Plenty wrong," Boyle sneered. "Mr. Warren is dead."

The only information I picked up was that Mr. Warren was found dead in a gully behind the house. Arthritis in the hip forced him to get around with a cane. He had fallen from the path into the gully, breaking his collar bone on the way down and smashing his skull against a boulder. A sixty-three year old man with arthritis can trip himself up pretty easily, but *did* he trip, I wondered, or was he helped along? At the moment death was attributed as accidental.

Boyle made no further attempt to hold me. We finished up at the patio and he told me to take off. I walked back to the car, slipped in behind the wheel, and then spotted the blonde coming my way. She was Diane Warren, the dead man's niece. The young man, was her brother Ralph.

I waited until she came up alongside and then gave her an inquiring glance. "You want to see me?" I asked.

"Why did my uncle want to see you?" she demanded.

"You heard what I told the police. I don't know."

"You're *lying!*"

Her eyes were icy blue, but I had the feeling that under different circumstances, and in the right place, they could warm up. I turned the key and hit the starter. The motor caught. I nodded and she stepped back as I pulled away.

I was glad to be on my way. There was that shower, and I hated to keep Carol waiting.

AT A LITTLE PAST TEN the phone rang. I was stretched

out on the sofa, my head in Carol's lap. She was able to get the receiver out of the cradle without getting up. After a moment she handed it to me.

"For you," she said impishly, "and she sounds pretty."

It was Diane Warren. She had called the office and my answering service had given her Carol's number. She had driven into town and was in her apartment. She wanted to see me.

"Why?"

"I'd rather not say over the phone."

I nodded toward the pad on the table and Carol passed it along with a pencil. I jotted down the address, and I heard the click on her end before I could say good-bye.

Carol helped me into my jacket and walked me to the door.

"Will you be back later?" she asked.

"It might be late."

"Have you ever been locked out yet?"

I kissed her alongside the neck. "I'll be back."

DIANE WARREN'S PLACE was in the East Sixties, one of those renovated brownstones. The carpeted hallway muffled my footsteps. I found her door and pressed the buzzer. She opened within ten seconds. She had undergone quite a change. Her hair was fluffed out and she was wearing some kind of lounging pajamas. She closed the door after me and led the way into the living room.

She poured me a drink and got to business. It occurred to her that I might have some notions about her uncle's death. If so, she wanted to assure me that I was sniffing a cold trail. Her uncle's death was an accident, pure and simple.

"And you dragged me up here to tell me that?"

She put her hand on my shoulder, then let it slide down my arm. "You think I'm spoiled, don't you?"

I was thinking something when the buzzer rang. It sounded exactly like a rattler. I turned to put my glass down when I heard her give a funny gasp from the door. When I straightened up they were moving toward me. They were big, tight-lipped and ugly.

The middle one wore his hat well down on what little forehead he had. His jaw was as thick as a mule's and he had a back to match. He shoved a stubby forefinger in my direction.

"You Baxter?"

"Adam Baxter," I corrected. "My mother called me Adam because I was the first of her bouncing brood. Mother had nineteen, bless her dear, sweet heart."

He fumbled over this for a few seconds, then his eyes went hard. He glanced up at his tall partner and nodded towards me. "A wise guy, no less."

The tall guy was no nonsense. He came in fast. I sidestepped, but not in time. He caught me alongside the cheekbone. As I reeled, muleface got in the fun. There was a chopping blow behind the ear, then another in the small of my back. Muleface must have worked his way around behind me. It had his touch. I was going down when the tall guy caught me by the lapels.

"Stay clear of the Warren business," he muttered. Then he let me fall.

I came to on the sofa with a cold compress on my head and a body full of aches.

"I don't know who they were," Diane protested. "That's the truth, Baxter."

I looked around dazedly. A tall guy with a sunburned face peered into mine. I turned to Diane.

"Who's he?"

"Dave Garett, my fiance." She made it sound like an apology. "He dropped by only a few minutes ago. After *they* left."

"You missed the fun," I whispered painfully. "Right, Diane?"

I slowly got to my feet.

"Can I drop you off?" Garett asked.

I shook my head. "You stay and talk with Diane."

She followed me to the door. "I'm sorry about what happened," she said. "But I had nothing to do with it."

I nodded.

"What about those men?" she whispered. "And their warning. You won't go looking for trouble. I'd hate to—"

I touched the goose egg under my eye very gently. "I had no intentions of messing around, but this changes things. I've got an investment going now. I'll be sticking around."

I CALLED CAROL and told her not to wait up, then I managed to get back to my place. I threw a piece of beefstake on my eye, an icebag on my head and rolled into bed. I felt better in the morning. Not a lot, but some. I got to the office after ten, just when the phone began to ring. It was Dan Walewski. He sounded like an old coot with a voice like a rusty hinge. Said he was Mr. Warren's handy man. He wanted to talk to me on Saturday, but he'd have no truck with them police "fellas". Would I come by that evening. It was mighty important.

I said I would.

I closed up shop after six and I headed for the Warren place.

I got there a little after seven, passed the main gate and went on to the turn-off about a hundred yards up. There was a second gate there, just like Walewski said. I pulled over, braked and got out. The gate had been left open and I followed the narrow path. I could see the shack through the trees. I knocked on the door. It was very still. I knocked again. It was partially open so I stepped inside. Dan Walewski was home, but he was on the floor. There was a bullet hole in his left temple. He was very, *very*, dead.

I made the usual search. There was nothing on the inside, but outside, behind the right corner of the shack, I found a few cigarette stubs. There was no brand name. Whoever had smoked them had opened the wrong end of the pack and lit up the trade-marked tip. There was a matchbook though. It carried the name of a "Village" nightspot, *"The Lark."* I had heard of the place. Its reputation was smelly. I pocketed the matchbook and headed back for the car. I was home around ten. I didn't go to Carol's. I wanted to think. *(Continued on next page)*

MESSAGE OF MURDER

THE FOLLOWING MORNING I gave Diane a call. She was pleasantly surprised, especially when I tossed in the luncheon invite.

"I'd love it," she cooed.

She was waiting outside when I drove up. I flipped open the door and she slipped in. There was a clouded look to her eyes.

"Let's have it," I said.

It was about Dan Walewski. She had heard about it only minutes after I called. A neighbour's dog had found the body and set up a howl. The police were called and notification followed.

When I straightened up they were moving toward me. They were big, tight-lipped and ugly.

She faced me. "Who would want to kill Dan?"

I said: "That's exactly what I wanted to know last night."

She gave me a funny look and I went on and explained about Dan's call and my going up to see him. "I wonder what he wanted to tell me?" I asked aloud.

She didn't answer. She sat with her hands folded in her lap until I pulled into the restaurant's parking lot.

We ordered cocktails and sipped them pretty much in silence. When the waiter left with our order I decided to make my move. I took out the matchbook I had found outside Dan's shack and put it down in front of her. "Ever been here?"

"You might as well 'fess up," I said. "Who do you know in *The Lark?*"

It came out piecemeal. She knew Nick Spanno, the owner. She had met him about a year back when some friends dropped by his place while hanging one on. She and Nick had become friendly. She was sketchy on the details, but she had become indebted to Nick. She had been placing some bets with him.

"What kind?"

"Horses."

I nodded. "And you've been running up a bill?"

It was her time to nod.

"How many *G's* you in for?"

The cloudy look returned. "I don't follow..."

"How much do you owe this Nick?" I demanded impatiently. Three... four... Five thousand?"

"About that. Maybe around five."

"Was he putting any presure on?"

She nodded again. "Some."

That was about the end of it. We finished on a quiet note and I dropped her off at her place. She invited me up and I reminded her about her fiance.

"Doesn't he mind? I mean your asking strange men up to your place."

Her hand was on my arm. "But you're no stranger."

I glanced toward the car. There was about five minutes on the meter. "I'm out of dimes," I said. "I'd better get going before they hang one on me."

She was still standing by the curb, watching me go, when I turned the corner.

IT WAS A LITTLE PAST EIGHT that night when I dropped in at *The Lark*. There was only a trickle of business and the cigarette smoke hadn't built up a fog. I took a table in the far corner and waited. A drug store redhead in a black, skin-tight dress showed up: one of the hostesses. She gave me the smile pitch and leaned forward. I didn't object. It was an improvement on the general view.

"Something I can do for you?" she asked.

"Yes," I said. "Go tell Nick I'd like to see him."

She straightened up. "Who shall I say?"

"Tell him Santa Claus." I laughed. "It's a joke," I explained. "Nick'll understand."

She disappeared through a rear door behind some phony palms. Pretty soon the door reopened and the three "muskateers" filed out with muleface in the lead. I wasn't really surprised. I touched the .45 tucked into my belt for luck. It was one hell of a morale booster.

The tall one, the one that clobbered me first at Diane's place, did the honors. "How come you wanna see Nick?"

I shrugged. "A business deal. I'm giving a private party." I looked around. "Maybe I should have it here—amongst friends."

Nick was a disappointment. He was short and bald. His complexion was the texture of mouldy cheese. The bad part was the mouth. There were no lips, just a thin, straight line.

He leaned forward across the desk. "What's your beef, Baxter? You got exactly *three* minutes."

"It seems you're holding a fistful of I.O.U.'s belonging to interested party."

He shrugged. "Is that all?"

"It could be more. You read the papers, Spanno. There's been a couple of deaths."

"So what. People die every day."

"That's not the right answer," I said.

The straight, thin line twitched. He nodded toward his goons. Only this time I was ready. Muleface caught it. I rammed the snub-nosed end of my automatic into his gut and he gasped like a punctured tire. I then shoved it under his chin.

"Make a move," I snapped, "and what little brains he has will be decorating your wallpaper."

His buddies froze. Muleface was whimpering. Nick gave me a long, solid stare. "You're way off, Baxter," he said. "I don't scare, and I could get you for this in my own time and in my own way. Only you've got the pitch all wrong. This isn't my kind of operation. My advice is put up and clear out."

There was no point to sticking around. I felt for the door behind me, turned the knob. Tucking the automatic back into my belt I slipped out.

I braked at the first corner and checked the street lamp. I was way off on Christopher Street. I began heading north. At Fourteenth I pulled up alongside an outdoor phone booth. I dialed and waited. It rang twice, then Diane answered. I did all the talking. I was taking a raincheck on her invitation. She could expect me at her place in twenty minutes. I hung up and was on my way.

She looked just a bit frightened when she answered my buzz.

"What's it all about?" she began.

I didn't give her a chance to think. I had her by the arms and gave it to her straight. "You've been lying." I growled. "Lying like crazy."

She shook her head. "About what?"

I didn't take to the bait. "What's the daily-double?" I snapped. "What month do they run the Derby?"

She was on the point of tears.

I gave her a few solid shakes. "You've been lying," I repeated. "Covering up. For who?"

I heard the slight noise from behind. I turned. There was only a small lamp on. The bedroom door was open and the dark, blurred figure sped for me. I saw the gleam of metal in his hand and I swung my body forward. I hit him across the groin with the flat of my hand and he doubled up. Then I came out of my crouch, leading with my right. It smashed into his mouth and he went limp. He toppled over without a sound.

Diane was at his side crying. I got up and brushed the hair from my eyes.

"Are you going to call the police?"

I nodded.

She looked at me through her tears. "I wanted to help him," she sobbed.

WRAP-UPS ARE usually anticlimactic. Ralph's story followed the pattern. The gambling debts were his and his uncle would come through. The inheritance seemed like the only thing, especially as Nick kept up the pressure. He bungled the first few tries and old man Warren gave me the buzz. Then the kid put through the finishing touch. Dan's killing was a messy follow-up. The old guy had spotted Ralph when he gave his uncle the final shove and so old Dan just had to go. In-so-far as Nick, like I thought, he was in just to protect his investment. And what about me? What was I in it for? There wasn't even a fee!

My body still ached when I got to Carol's that night. She got out the liniment and went to work.

"When were you sure that Diane Warren was lying about those racing bets?" she asked.

I yawned. "When I remembered our conversation we had at lunch. I asked her how many *G's* she was in for to Spanno and I drew a blank. Now what gambler wouldn't know what a *G* is?"

Carol grinned. "Not knowing any gamblers, I wouldn't know."

I reached up and pulled her down beside me. That's when the phone rang. She started to reach for it and I took her hand.

"Let it ring," I said.

"Whatever you say," she whispered. "You're *boss!*"

THE END

Dangerous Curves

(Continued from page 15)

THAT NIGHT I WAS draped over a bar stool as fetchingly as possible in the Santa Ynez Inn, a beach spot in Santa Monica. It was O'Farrell's favorite hangout. I had donned my hunting clothes—a simple black cocktail dress that fitted close and was slashed to the waist in front.

I waited patiently and about 10 o' clock Jeff and his little brunette wiggler came in. He was a big good-looking guy with brown curly hair, real muscles and real sex appeal.

The gal with him wasn't bad. She had a provocative full-lipped pout and roving black eyes. She had on too much make-up, but that was all she had on too much of. She wore a white dress that looked like it was a size smaller than her skin.

They sat down at the bar, three stools away. He sat on the side of her that put him nearest to me, and I decided I had scored once.

"Hey, Sweetie, are you with me or not?" she hissed angrily at Jeff. "Or would you rather sit and ogle that blonde all night?"

"I'm sorry, Honey. I just recognized somebody I've seen on the lot. I didn't mean to stare. Don't get mad."

"Well, I'm ready to leave this joint," Carla snarled. I'm going to the powder room, and then I want to take off.

And with that she slid off her stool and undulated across the floor with a walk that turned every male head in the place.

He turned back to me with the most appealing grin this side of the old Shirley Temple movies.

"I have seen you around the lot, haven't I?" he asked.

Then he thought to ask my name, and I said, "Liz, just Liz. And I'll be leaving here alone..."

"I can make it alright," he said. "I'll be back in exactly one hour—that'll be 12:15. Okay?"

(Continued on page 44)

Dangerous Curves

(Continued from page 43)

* Private Eye

"It's a date: I'll be in my car, the white Thunderbird on the far side of the parking lot," I whispered as I saw Carla coming back.

But, even though she looked mad, she didn't come directly toward us. She stopped at a table in the corner to talk to three gangster types who were sitting taking in everything—especially me.

I wanted to get a closer look at them, so I murmured, "See you later"

Carla steamed through the door right behind me and grabbed my arm.

"Say, what's the idea?" she grated at me. "Who the hell do you think you're cutting in on?"

With a string of obscenities, Carla made a grab for my face, long lacquered fingernails out. But little Liz hadn't forgotten her training as a police woman. I caught her wrist neatly and pulled her by me, twisting her into a helpless and painful arm lock. She screamed, and the powder room woman and a couple of others rushed over babbling.

I played it cool before the other astonished women and pulled out my powder puff and dabbed carefully at my nose. I had to figure what to do next. I was sure Carla's tough playmates would be waiting for me when I went back out.

I didn't want to get dragged off and worked over by them without even making contact with their boss.

I LOOKED OUT and realized I'd gotten a break. The waiter was just seating two couples at the table right next to the two roughnecks. They could not move now. I swiveled blithely by with a pleased smile on my face, and got a couple of admiring glances from the guys in the new party.

Then one of them went out toward the door and the other came over to the bar stool next to mine.

"Hey Baby, can I buy you a drink," he growled.

"Thanks, but I've got a fresh one right here," I answered. "But speak up. What's on your mind?"

"Lookie here. Whatcha tryin' to chisel in on this other girl's fella for. Now you're a good-lookin' broad. You could get lots of guys. Whatcha wanta make trouble for?"

He leered down at my cleavage.

I let him look. I didn't move. I was busy thinking, wondering whether I could get him to take me to Ambrazza right then.

"Look Buster," I said, "I'm not trying to marry Jeff O'Farrell and take him out of circulation, and I don't want to cut out your girl, whatever her game is, but he's the biggest, handsomest, most important movie star in the country, and a girl like me, who wants to get ahead, can't afford to lose a contact like that if she has a chance to make one.

"You don't need O'Farrell," he said. "My boss can help you. He's a producer. And he'd go for a good-looking, smart dame like you."

"Well, seeing is believing," I smiled.

I talked him into making a date for tomorrow night at the same place and he went off, his suspicions pretty well allayed.

AT 12:15 I WENT OUT to the Thunderbird and got in. I spotted my two gorillas lurking in a Chrysler sedan on the other side of the parking lot, but they made no move, so I didn't either. Sure enough, in about three minutes, a white Jaguar convertible

---

Solution to the: "CARR CASE MYSTERY"

The distance of Carr's toes above the floor was several inches greater than the height of the overturned chair. If Carr had hung himself, this distance would have been the same.

Bailey confessed under pressure. He strangled his partner, then hung him from the beam to look like suicide. Motive? To own their business in full.

Bailey was convicted and is serving a life sentence.

* Private Eye

spun into the lot and up beside me and Jeff O'Farrell uncoiled his big frame from behind the wheel.

"Climb in," I invited with a big smile.

We made a series of clubs and bars in fast succession.

Then went into my apartment

As soon as we were inside I went to the window and opened it and stood long enough so the gorillas would see me. When Jeff came over to kiss me, I let him, and I put my all in it.

I unclinched us, and said, "How about that drink?"

After I gave him his drink and had mine, I flipped the lamp down to its lowest setting and wandered by the window. I was just in time to see the sedan pulling off. They had seen enough.

Jeff was on the sofa.

"Aren't you going to sit down," he said. "What's the matter, don't you like me?"

"Of course I do," I said, slipping down beside him.

"But I can't let you stay all night. My reputation, you know. Also, what if your girl Carla got wind of this?"

"She doesn't own me," Jeff replied. "I want to see some more of you."

I assured him he would, and wandered by the window to look out. My own reference to Carla had reminded me that the hoods might be back. Sure enough, they were. And, I got a shock. There were three in the car now. This might be my big break. If the third one was Ambrazza himself, I might have a chance to make a real coup before morning.

Poor Jeff was a little upset that he couldn't talk me into a romance, but I insisted I was just dead tired, he made a date for the next day for cocktails.

I watched from behind closed blinds as he went down to the street, hailed a cab and departed. The three in the sedan got out and entered my building.

It was going to be touch and go, and I might end up with my girlish beauty mashed into a bloody pulp, but I had to chance it. I put the little automatic in the deep pocket of my terry cloth bathrobe, and set my tape recorder going in its hidden panel behind my hi-fi set. The buzzer rang.

My heart jumped when I opened the door. The third man was my pidgeon, Nick Ambrazza. The guy who had been at the bar with earlier grabbed my arm and dragged me into the room.

"All right Baby, talk fast. What's your game? I don't have much patience with smart little girls who play dumb."

"What do you mean, what's my game? What's yours? You trying to blackmail Jeff O'Farrell or something with this little brunette tart? Why should you care if I make a little time with Jeff."

"I told you to lay off him," the gorilla who had been at the bar growled. "Shall I work her over to teach her, boss?" he asked Ambrazza.

Nick signalled him back, and peered at me intently, trying to make up his mind. I held my breath, waiting to see if I had convinced him.

Suddenly Nick smiled. "You're a pretty cute chick," he said. "I don't want to get rough with you. I could go for you myself.

"But you've got it wrong. You know who I am, and you think I'm out here to do something terrible. You talk about blackmail. But you're all wrong Baby. Nick's no criminal. I'm gonna be a movie producer. In fact, Jeff is gonna be my biggest star. That's the reason I take an interest in him. But that's all. Nothing wrong about that."

My heart was pounding. This was almost enough on the tape, but I needed a little more of the details. Enough so I could convince Jeff, and maybe have evidence of Nick's intention to commit criminal fraud.

"So what are you pushing me around for?" I asked, with the hint of a sob in my voice. "I'm not going to crab your deal or hurt Jeff. Everybody makes promises and wants to sleep with you, but they get mad if you want to get a lousy little part and get ahead. He could help me.

"Look Kid, take it easy. I told you I'd help you," Nick said. "I really will. Only stay away from him. I tell you what, suppose we have dinner tomorrow, and I'll start right away. I'll really do things for you."

His hand roamed down my shoulder and bare arm.

"I still don't understand why you're picking on me, and watching out so carefully to see that that little black-haired dame gets O'Farrell. What is she—a relative of yours?"

"Her," he burst out, "a relative of mine? Nah, she's only a call girl from our Chicago set-up. She's getting Jeff

(Continued on page 46)

BOSOMS and BULLETS
(Continued from page 38)

Peltner. Boy they sure looked good to me in anything, or nothing. About eight that night we were ready to leave, when one important thing dawned on me. Being an escort, and although I wouldn't be going inside, I'd still feel out of place if I didn't have a penguin suit on. The girls agreed, and it was decided that they would escort me to my Greenwich Village apartment for a fast change before we went to the shindig.

I must admit that after glancing at myself in the mirror, I cut a pretty handsome figure. Although, when I occasionally looked down, my beard hid the tie. "Lets go my two beauties." "Girls, I think we'll have to walk to the main street and hop a cab there. How's about me carrying those models bags for you. No sense in you kids lugging it."

"No, no, Sam. We are used to it. In fact we would feel naked if we didn't carry these bags."

"As you wish. C'mon, let's take a short cut through this alley. It'll bring us out on Sixth Avenue. Boy, it's a nice peaceful night."

I felt a whistle past my ear, and a chunk of building flew past my nose. And as I threw both girls to the side, I cursed at myself for being so clumsy and taken in with my clients and the night air. I could tell when someone was throwing lead my way, and man, it was coming fast.

"GET DOWN and stay there, keep behind me, and don't start craning your necks to get a better view, or someor else out there may use it for target practice."

I caught a glimpse of a shadow looking out from behind a parked car. A shadow with a luger in his hand. I took careful aim and squeezed the trigger. His scream was good enough to tell me I haven't lost my touch. A moment later the starting of

(Continued on page 49)

SEX Is What You Make It!

ONLY $1.98

Your "sexcess" depends on when, where, how, how much, with whom—and a lot more. It calls for the right line and the sure touch. And what you don't know can hurt you!

EVERY DETAIL PICTURE-CLEAR
Lay questions, doubts and fears to rest. Get straightened out and "cued up" with the best-selling FROM FREUD TO KINSEY, now in its ninth large printing. All the answers you need in plain man-and-woman talk—every detail picture-clear! Exciting entertainment from cover to cover!

ORDER ON APPROVAL
Order FROM FREUD TO KINSEY in plain wrapper for 10 days FREE examination. If not completely satisfied, return it for immediate refund of purchase price. Don't go another night without it!

10 DAY FREE TRIAL · MAIL COUPON NOW

```
PLAZA BOOK CO., Dept. K-1411
109 Broad St., New York 4, N. Y.
Rush FROM FREUD TO KINSEY in plain wrapper
for 10 DAY FREE TRIAL. If not satisfied, I get my
purchase price refunded at once.
☐ Send C.O.D. I'll pay postman $1.98 plus postage.
☐ I enclose $1.98. You pay all postage.
Name.................................Age.........
Address..........................................
City..............Zone.....State............
Canada & Foreign—No C.O.D.—Send $2.50
```

HAND TIED FISHING FLIES
12 for $1.00 post paid
Only the finest genuine feathers and materials are used by our skilled craftsmen. 12 popular patterns, packed in a fine compact wood box with cork retainers. Send $1.00 cash, check or money order to
PANTHER FLY Dept. 53
45 W. 45th St. N.Y.C 36

CLASSIFIED OPPORTUNITIES

FOR WOMEN
MAKE $25 to $35 weekly addressing envelopes. Our instructions reveal how. Glenway, Box 6568, Cleveland 1, Ohio.

$3.00 Hour. Average earnings, assembling pump lamps. Simple, Easy. Selling not required. Write Ougor, Trilby 5, Florida.

HOME SEWERS
HOME SEWERS! Earn $50.00 weekly sewing spare time. No canvassing Readykit's, Loganville, Wisconsin

FOR PHOTO FANS
HIGH CASH PRICES paid for unusual, odd, photographs. Market details for stamp Portraits, Box 885, Washington 4, D C

HYPNOTISM
HYPNOTIZE SELF, OTHERS while asleep with amazing hypnotic phonograph records, tapes. Catalog free. Sleep-Learning Research Association, Box 24-CO, Olympia, Washington.

U.S. & FOREIGN JOB LISTINGS
AMERICAN OVERSEAS JOBS High pay Men, Women. Transportation paid Free Information Transworld, Dept. BG, 200 West 34th St, New York 1, N Y

SALESMEN WANTED
BUSINESS KIT FREE! Postcard puts you in business! Complete line 230 shoe styles, also jackets! New discoveries pay big commissions. No investment. Send for free kit. Mason, Chippewa Falls M-7, Wisconsin

BUSINESS OPPORTUNITY
$30-$60 WEEKLY addressing envelopes for advertisers. Instructions $1, refundable. Ryco Service, 210 Fifth Ave. Suite 1102-F New York 10

IDEAL SIDELINE Contact doctors, druggists, service stations, taverns, etc Full or part time. Latex drug sundries lowest prices, top profits, popular brands Send $2.00 for sample kit Write for free details. Federal Pharmacal Supply Inc. Dept. MG, 6640 N Western Ave Chicago 45, Ill

SCHOOLS & INSTRUCTIONS
LEARN CIVIL AND criminal investigation at home. Earn steady, good pay Institute Applied Science, 1920 Sunnyside, Dept. 247, Chicago 40, Illinois

Dangerous Curves
(Continued from page 45)

O'Farrell to sign for me. That's the reason I'm making sure nobody gets in her way. Now do you understand?

He'd said it. Everything I needed was on the tape now. I almost burst out laughing.

"We'll have a date tomorrow, then, and you'll really help me," I said.

"Yeah, but never mind tomorrow," he said, pulling me against him. "What's the matter right now?"

"No," I said, acting shy. "After we know each other..."

"What's this 'after' business?" he exploded, dragging me down to the sofa.

"No," I said, struggling, and when he wouldn't let go of my arm, my bathrobe was pulled off one shoulder again and half off me and I got mad and slapped him.

That was the mistake. He hit me hard, with his fist, and for a minute I saw stars as the sofa floated up and I fell across the arm of it onto the floor, dizzy. He reached for me again. I was just aware of one thing beside my spinning head and that was a sharp bruise on my fanny as I landed legs in the air all wound up in the bathrobe. Then I realized the hard bruising object under me was the gun in the pocket of the robe

I groped for it with my right hand as he pulled me to my feet by my left arm. Then I had it out and between us, and he saw it.

"Let go of me," I yelled. But he grabbed for the pistol.

The little gun made a pretty loud noise, but fortunately his hoods had gone all the way back to the car. He spun back abruptly and sat down on the floor, blood coming from under the hand he held to his side. People came running, and his thugs took off when they heard the police siren.

The authorities gave Nick his choice of getting out of the state or facing a host of minor charges when he was out of the hospital. He went back east. The tape was enough to convince Jeff O'Farrell that he was being taken for a sucker.

Zenith Studios gave me a $1,000 bonus in addition to my fat $5,000 fee. And Cy Raymond even offered me a movie contract, but I turned it down. I felt flattered though.

When we broke it all to Jeff, he was amazed.

*Private Eye

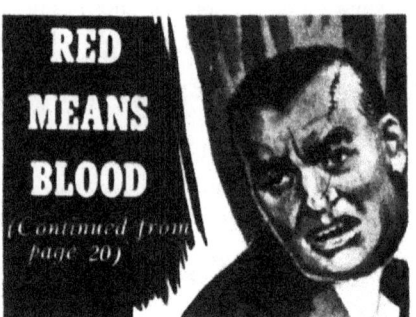

RED MEANS BLOOD
(Continued from page 20)

As Randall collected keys, cash and cigarettes into the pockets of his tan linen sport jacket he picked up the house phone and called downstairs to the garage twenty floors below.

"George, this is Mr. Randall. Have my car on the ramp. I'm on my way down."... "No, not the Caddie, the T-bird. Thanks George."

At twelve-fifteen A.M. the "Bird" was wheeling through lower Broadway and into the lanes approaching the ferry slip. Randall braked before the toll-gate, passed over the sixty-five cents for a ticket and bumped aboard the old boat that was waiting with its blunt end against the dock.

Randall eased out of the Thunderbird and crossed over into the yellow light of the passageway, through the swinging doors and up the steps to the top deck

In the main cabin he saw the neon-lighted snack bar, two drunks asleep on the slatted benches and an old scrubwoman reading a dog-eared tabloid on her way home from a night's work. But no sign of Nick Warden.

Randall walked down the long, brightly lighted aisle and sat down on a stool at the counter. "Coffee and a cruller," he told the sleepy counterman.

Still no sign of Warden. As the coffee was sloshed down in front of him Randall noticed that where there had been two drunks asleep on the benches now there was only one. The second man was walking unsteadily towards the counter. The unshaven

"The attention you got doesn't go with every case I handle," I grinned.

A broad smile broke over his big handsome face.

"Then maybe you'll go out with me tonight

"Okay," I replied, "and now it's on my own time, so what more can you ask?" THE END

* Private Eye

derelict, in a patched and faded denim jacket and nondescript trousers sat down next to Randall and pulled the ragged straw hat away from his face.

It was Nick Warden.

"It's been a long time Mark."

"It certainly has Nick. And from all the earmarks of this meeting it looks as though we're going to do more than just visit with each other for a while."

"Give the man a cigar," cracked Warden. "I know you aren't in the service Mark and haven't been for ten years now. But you are in the reserves and I've volunteered you for a quick job that needs doing.

Randall blinked in disbelief but knew that if Warden had chosen him there must be good reason.

"What needs doing, Nick?" asked Randall.

"Good. I'm glad you're with us." Warden paused, shifted around on the counter stool and then motioned Randall to follow him. They stepped quickly out onto the open deck and faced into the cool summer's breeze.

"Do you remember Irene Tedescu?" Randall nodded. He certainly did remember the beautiful, red-haired and green-eyed Irene who ten years ago as a girl just out of her teens had been one of the top Red agents in Berlin.

Warden continued.

"She's coming over to our side and she's bringing along a full list of red espionage agents working in the U.S. and Canada. We've had only one message from her. She's due in this morning aboard the new Italian luxury liner that'll pass Ambrose light in the Outer Bay at about 4:15 a.m. She's not a passenger but she's working as a manicurist in the First Class Men's Barber Shop.

"Mark, we've got to get her off and we have to lay our hands on those other agents aboard that ship who don't want our pretty little pigeon to start cooing."

Warden took a breath and went on with his story.

"Mark we have arranged for you to get out to the ship as a Health Inspector with the Coast Guard people when the boat stops in quarantine.

"We picked you Mark, because Irene knows you and knows that you're one of us. Once you've got her off the boat you've got to get her to your apartment. You remember Jeff Walsh?... good... he'll be in your

(Continued on page 48)

SAVE 75% on WORK CLOTHES!

Terrific Values You've Got To See To Believe!

SHIRTS 79c
4 for $2.99
What a buy! Made to sell for 2.99. Now, get 4 for the price of one! Tho used, they're washed, sterilized, pressed, and ready for long, tough wear! In blue, tan or green.
Send neck size, 1st and 2nd color choice.

MEN'S COVERALLS $2.29
Wear'em used and save plenty! You can't beat this bargain anywhere! The best made. Sold for 6.95. Now... wow!... what savings!
3 for $6.75
Send chest measurement.

Unlined WORK JACKETS 99c
3 for $2.75
Popular Eisenhower type. Four pockets. Heavy-weight twill. In good, solid condition for plenty of rugged wear! Blue only.
Send chest measurement.

PANTS 99c
to match   4 for $3.75
Think of it! Heavy-duty cotton twill pants that sold for 3.85! Now, fully reconditioned and yours at this rock-bottom price!
Send waist measure and inside leg length.

SHOP COATS—Like brand new! $1.79
3 for $5.00
Send chest measurement.

LADIES' COVERALLS—Though used, in perfect condition! $1.49
3 for $4.00
Send dress size.

MONEY BACK GUARANTEE... If not satisfied! That's our way of doing business! You can't lose! So order TODAY. Send $1.00 deposit on C.O.D. orders. Add 25c for postage on prepaid orders.

GALCO SALES CO. Dept. 3711
7120 HARVARD AVENUE • CLEVELAND 5, OHIO

A PLAYBOY WALLET

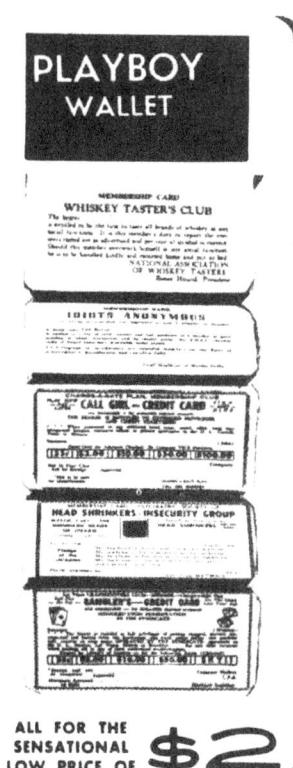

PLAYBOY WALLET

ALL FOR THE SENSATIONAL LOW PRICE OF $2
Sold with money back guarantee
SORRY NO C.O.D.'s

in silky black patent leather, imprinted PLAYBOY in large gold letters. Ten humorous cards of charter membership in the most unique and private Playboy clubs in the world.

- Whiskey Taster's Club
- Idiots Anonymous
- Call Girl Credit Card
- Head Shrinkers Insecurity Group
- Gambler's Credit Card
- The Pistol Club
- Alcoholics Unanimous
- Back Seat Driver's License
- Who Am I?—Card
- Permit of Freedom

EVERY PLAYBOY'S SURVIVAL WALLET
No man should be without one! Wonderful to give as gifts

Dept. 9N
Casanovas' Gifts and Gags
24 West 45th Street, New York 36, N. Y.
PLEASE FIND ENCLOSED $_____ FOR
( ) PLAYBOY SURVIVAL WALLET(S)
☐ CHECK ☐ CASH ☐ MONEY ORDER
Name _____
Address _____
City-State _____

Miss CUDDLE-UP pillowcase in full color
☐ Blonde
☐ Brunette
☐ Redhead
only $2.95 each or 2 for $5.00
Sorry, no C.O.D's
CUDDLE-UP Dept. PE, 550 5th Ave. New York 36, N.Y.

ILLUSTRATED BOOKLETS
The kind YOU will enjoy. Each one of these booklets is size 3½ by 4½ and is ILLUSTRATED with 8 page cartoon ILLUSTRATIONS of COMIC CHARACTERS and is full of fun and entertainment. 20 of these booklets ALL DIFFERENT sent prepaid in a plain envelope upon receipt of $1.00. No checks or C.O.D. orders accepted.
TREASURE NOVELTY CO. Dept. 22-A
182 Knickerbocker Station   New York 2, N.Y.

RED MEANS BLOOD

place when you get there. We've got our men on the doors in the elevators and in the garage of your building. Everything should be okay, Mark, once you get inside. There's going to be a white ambulance waiting at dockside for you to use as a cover car. One of my men will be driving. Any questions?"

"Only one," said Randall. "Am I dreaming all of this?"

"You're not dreaming buddy. This is so real in fact that you could get yourself killed. You can back away

"I'm in," said Randall. "Wish me luck. I'll need it in the next few hours."

WHEN THE FERRY DOCKED, Randall drove the Thunderbird up and over the ramp, pushed hard uphill for a fast quarter-mile and raced across the island. He hit an open stretch and then the straightaway leading to Outerbridge Crossing. Across the long span and then onto the Jersey flats reeking with chemical stench Randall pushed the Bird hard until he hit the tunnel to New York.

By one-thirty a.m. he was back in N.Y. and heading east on garishly lighted Forty-Second St., past Times Square and over east to the River.

"Nothing to do now but wait," thought Randall. He picked up the mobile phone under the dash and called his answering service. He left a message to notify his office that all morning appointments were to be cancelled if he was not in at his usual time. Randall put the phone back into its cradle, drew out a silver cigarette case and lit up. As he smoked he loaded half a dozen extra clips for the Webley from a cartridge box in the dash and shoved them into loops in his shoulder sling.

At four a.m. the T-Bird passed through the gate of the Coast Guard Pier on the East River. Customs and Immigration men were assembling to board the cutter going out to meet the incoming liner.

Randall walked into the pre-fab hut, picked up a mug of coffee on a raw wooden table under a sign that read "Help Yourself," and headed for the door marked "Chief Health Inspector."

The gilt lettered sign on the scarred desk read, "A. M. Goldberg, Chief. U.S. Health Service." Goldberg was standing over a yellowed sink in his undershirt scraping off a beard. "You

must be Randall," he asked, looking Mark over from his view in the mirror. "I'm Abe Goldberg. I'm not going to ask what's up but that doesn't mean I'm not curious as hell."

Mark liked the big man's manner and chuckled. Goldberg shrugged a shoulder towards a metal locker and said, "You'll find a uniform in there and all of your Health Service credentials are in the inside pocket."

At five-thirty a.m., just as the grey light was starting to uncover the misty skyline of lower Manhattan, the Coast Guard cutter drew alongside the Italian liner out in the bay. Lines were secured and ladders put down for the inspectors and reporters. On the way up the ladder Goldberg told Randall, "You're on your own buddy boy." Mark squeezed the big man's shoulder affectionately and hoisted himself aboard the liner. Sub-officers of the ship were waiting at the head of the ladder to escort officials to the checkpoints. Randall looked at one and said, "Crew's quarters—female."

"Follow me, please," said the young, blue-capped seaman.

They headed for the stern and the lower decks. In the crew's dining room a table and chairs had been set up and the chambermaids, beauticians and other female employees were waiting to be cleared to go ashore.

Randall sat down and picked up the list on the table. "As I call your name please step up and show your health cards."

He started reading the roll and one by one the women stepped forward and showed their innoculation cards as Randall stamped them "O.K."

The line moved fast and within half an hour he was down to the names starting with "T." Randall's eyes scanned the room but still he saw no sign of the woman he was looking for. Even in this crowd she would have been a standout. He continued calling names... "Tebaldi, Techanowski, Tedder." They kept filing up to the table. Then he called Tedescu...

none appeared. He called it again, his eyes searching the room, and still none came up. Randall called the name a third time and a woman he hadn't noticed before stepped up to the table and dropped a health card marked "Tedescu, Irene." But Randall knew this wasn't Irene. He stamped the card and asked another Health officer who had come in a few minutes earlier to relieve him.

Randall waved a smiling thanks to the officer and walked out of the cabin. The girl who had presented Irene Tedescu's card was gone. Randall thought fast. If Irene had been able to, she would have presented that card herself. But instead someone else had done it.

Randall flipped the pages of his copy of the crew list and read down until he saw Tedescu: A # 432. He sprinted around the deck and down three flights to "A Deck" until he came to # 432. Randall knew that in setups like this two cabins usually shared one bathroom. He counted off even numbers from where the passageway began and decided that # 434 and # 432 shared the same bath. He tried the door of # 434 and it came open easily. None was in the room and he locked the hallway door behind him. Stepping quietly, Randall loosened his uniform belt and unlimbered the .38. Without a sound he opened the bathroom door.

THE MUSKY ODOR of steam and bath oils hit him in the face. The tub was full and just ready to be used but none was in it. The door to the next room, Irene's room, was ajar.

Mark drew his gun and kicked the door open. He jumped into the room in a crouch as a woman screamed. She wasn't Irene. It was the girl who had presented Irene's card to Randall ten minutes earlier at the health check.

The lean, long legged brunette standing in panties with her hands busy with bra hooks spun around in surprise when she heard the door open and saw Randall standing there.

With a throaty and angry Italian voice she asked, "Is this part of a health inspector's job?" Her deep black eyes glared at Randall but he wasn't looking at the eyes.

Tauntingly she let the bra fall and twisted her lush olive-skinned body for Randall to see. "Am I healthy enough, Mr. Inspector," she laughed.

His eyes misted as he looked at the

beautiful body and seconds passed without a sound. Then she screamed at him, "Now get out of here, pig." Her anger turned into a warm and teasing smile and she added... "... but maybe you come back later."

"No," said Randall, coming back to his senses, all I want is an answer to one question.

"I bet I know what that question is," said the girl as she walked with arched back to the bathroom door where Randall was standing. "Never mind," said Randall, smiling, "you've already answered THAT question. I have another one."

She pouted and looked confused then Randall shot, "Where is Irene Tudescu?"

The girl twisted towards Randall again put her arms around his neck and rubbed the tips of her breasts against his chest. "You like Irene more maybe?"

Randall took another look at the woman against him and answered, "No, I no like Irene more but I still want to know where she is."

The brunette spun away and threw herself across the bed, her long black hair spreading against the white sheets
(Continued on page 50)

BOSOMS and BULLETS

Continued from page 45

a motor and the screaming of tires told me the boys weren't hanging around. I ducked out of the alley and looked around. People had heard the shots and were coming out from all directions. Even a cabbie who heard the shots, inquisitively pulled up. I grabbed the girls by the arm and hustled them in.

"Hotel Beauxley driver."

Traffic was pretty heavy at that hour, and the cabbie was gabby all the way uptown. I hardly had a chance to discuss this attack with my two beauties. It began to strike me pretty odd that someone would go to all this trouble to try and knock off two witnesses to a murder that hasn't been publicized. If there was a murder. I would have to be more on my guard.

THE LOBBY OF THE HOTEL was sure swank. It was filled with the cream of society, and enough ice to make a skating rink. I actually felt like one of them as I escorted my two beauties toward the elevator.

"Hey Sam" I turned at a familiar gruff voice. "If it isn't Lieutenant Cy Jackson, the only beatnik cop on the force." Cy was a good detective, and also a good friend. We both had a few things in common. Good art and good music. My style, of course. "Sam, I looked up the who's who, and social register, and by jimminy, I must've overlooked your name."

"You flatter me Cy, but I have been retained by these packages of loveliness from South America to escort them here and then to their plane. You know, admirers getting too friendly and such."

I introduced the girls to Cy.

"My sister Maria and I are pleased to meet you Mr. Jackson.

I gave Cy the wise guy look and entered the elevator with my clients.
(Continued on page 64)

MEAT CUTTING OFFERS YOU
SUCCESS And SECURITY

In The Best Established Business In The World • PEOPLE MUST EAT!

Students (above) getting actual practice training in meat cutting in only their 3rd day at school. Students (below) getting actual practice training on power saw. Students train on all the latest power tools and equipment.

TRAIN QUICKLY in 8 short weeks for a job with a bright and secure future in the vital meat business. Trained meat men needed. Good pay, full-time jobs, year-round income, no lay-offs—HAVE A PROFITABLE MARKET OF YOUR OWN!

LEARN BY DOING

Get your training under actual meat market conditions in our big, modern, cutting and processing rooms and retail meat market. Expert instructors show you how—then you do each job yourself. Nearly a million dollars worth of meat is cut, processed, displayed and merchandised by National students yearly!

PAY AFTER GRADUATION

Come to National for complete 8-weeks course and pay your tuition in easy installments after you graduate. Diploma awarded. FREE nationwide employment help. Thousands of successful graduates. OUR 36th YEAR!

FREE CATALOG—MAIL COUPON

Send coupon for big, fully illustrated, National School catalog showing students in training. See for yourself what rapid progress you can make. See meat you cut and equipment you train with. No obligation. No salesman will call. FOR REAL JOB SECURITY, get all the facts NOW! G.I. Approved.

National School Of Meat Cutting
Dept. PE-10   Toledo 4, Ohio

NATIONAL SCHOOL OF MEAT CUTTING, Dept. PE-10   Toledo 4, Ohio
Send me your FREE illustrated school catalog showing me how I can quickly train for SUCCESS and SECURITY in Meat Cutting, Meat Merchandising and Self Service Meats. No obligation. No salesman will call. Approved for veterans.
Name...Age............
Address...
City...Zone........State.......................

AMAZING!
FIGURE SLIMMER

NOW offered for the first time

ONLY 3.49 complete with crotch piece

The New Combination Adjustable Waist and Abdominal Leveler

Slenderizes Both Abdomen and Waist
Figure Slimmer corrects the faults of other garments. Some hold in the stomach but push out the waist. Figure Slimmer slenderizes both the waist and abdominal appearance at the same time. You will look inches slimmer and feel wonderful.

Holds Back Together
Figure Slimmer is wonderful for that falling-apart back feeling. Its firm, gentle compressing action makes you feel good and secure.

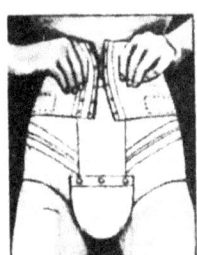

Appear Inches Slimmer
Figure Slimmer flattens your front and takes in inches off your appearance. Clothes will look well on you now!

Adjustable
Figure Slimmer's adjustable feature makes it easy for you to have a small waistline look. Trousers now look good and fit swell. You can take yourself in more inches if you wish, with this novel adjustable feature. Try 10 days!

TRY 10 DAYS FREE

Ward Green Co., 43 W. 61 St., N.Y. 23 Dept. P-761

Rush for ten days approval the new Figure Slimmer. After wearing for ten days, I can return it for full refund of purchase price if not satisfied.

☐ Send C.O.D. I will pay postman plus postage.
☐ I enclose $3.49. Send it prepaid. ($3.98 for waist 46 and up.) EXTRA crotch pieces, 50¢ each.

My waist measure is _____ inches.

NAME
ADDRESS
CITY   ZONE   STATE

RED MEANS BLOOD

beneath her. She pouted and shrugged her shoulders. "She share cabin with me but last night she not sleep here." The woman moved provocatively and giggled, "Maybe she have boyfriend on ship?"

"When did you see her last," asked Randall. "Was about 11 o'clock last night," said the girl growing serious as she saw the determination in Mark's eyes. "Chief Steward came and ask Irene if she mind making manicure for big shot passenger in first class suite for ten dollar. Irene say she not want to go and I say for ten dollars I go. But steward he say passenger asked for Irene and that she better go or no liberty in New York. So, Irene, she go."

"What cabin did she go to," asked Mark. The girl looked at him and said, "Irene is my friend and maybe that none of your business." Randall's eyes narrowed and he moved toward the bed where she was stretched out. "I'm making it my business," he said between clenched teeth. "If you don't tell me I'll put black and blue patches all over that beautiful skin of your's."

"Okay tough guy, okay." She reached over to a nightstand and handed Randall a slip of paper. "Here's paper with Cabin number that Steward give Irene last night."

Randall looked at the slip and saw "Boat Deck, Suite F" scrawled across the paper. "Thanks," said Randall "now you can finish what you were doing." The brunette rolled over on her back, ran her hands across her naked breasts and softly breathed, "I like to finish with you big man." Randall looked back with a promise in his eyes as he slipped out of the room.

HE SPRINTED FORWARD and then up three gangways to the Boat Deck. In front of Suite F he paused for a moment and then knocked.

"Ja, who iss dere?" asked a gruff, heavily accented voiced from behind the door. "U.S. Health Inspector," shouted Randall. "Already been inspected," growled the voice as feet shuffled towards the door. "Never mind," answered Randall, drawing his gun again, "I have to ask some more questions."

The door swung open and a giant of a man filled the doorway. Randall punched the barrel of his .38 into the flab of the giant's belly and said, "Step back and don't make a sound if you want to live." The bald giant's face froze in terror as he did what Warden ordered.

A voice from the bedroom called out in Russian, "What was that all about?" Randall understood enough Russian from his Berlin days and whispered to the quivering giant in front of him. "Tell him nothing, nothing at all." The man uttered the words and stared down at the silver blue barrel probing into the folds of flesh below his waistline.

Randall looked up at the man. Through clenched teeth he asked, "Is the Tedescu girl in there?" The giant's eyes darted around frantically and he stuttered, "No gurrl, Iss no gurl dere." Randall drove the hard steel of the gun barrel deeper into the man's belly and pulled the hammer back with his thumb. Eyes wide open, the big man gasped, ". . . no kill, please no kill me. Gurrl iss inside . . ."

Randall shoved him around and walked him to the bedroom door. The man shaking and in a cold sweat, moved as though he was a robot. "Now open it," said Randall pointing to the door and hiding his own six feet behind the man's hulk.

A blaze of gunfire ripped through the stillness of the suite as half a dozen slugs tore into the fatty flesh of the body shielding Randall. As the giant's groaning body started to fall Mark hand-pumped the Webley at the gunman. The smoking automatic fell to the floor as the man spun to the floor with blood pumping out of a head wound.

Randall smashed into the stateroom and in a short exchange of fire instanly killed the gunman who just shot his comrade full of holes.

Mark spotted the beautiful Irene Tedescu tied into a wheel chair in the corner, a bloody gag stuffed into her mouth.

Her eyes stared up at Randall in open disbelief as he pulled the gag away. "You," she breathed. "After all of these years!" Randall smiled but only for a second as the look of surprise on the girl's face turned to one of cold terror.

Mark didn't move but he felt someone behind him.

"That's right, Mr. Randall, do not move or I will kill you immediately," rasped a heavily accented voice.

Randall dropped his still smoking Webley and the man moved around to

* Private Eye

face him. It was Karl von Jurgund who Randall had known as an SS butcher in Nazi days and now in the pay of the reds.

The German smirked. "And so Herr Randall we meet again, ja? But this time is different, no?"

"No," said Randall, "you are in American territory and you won't get away. We'll get you and you'll be shipped back to Western Germany where you'll be tried and maybe even hanged as a war criminal."

Von Jurgund's face darkened and bubbles ran from the corners of his mouth. "I won't be caught Mr. Randall and I won't be tried. But even if I were it would give you no satisfaction because in less than thirty seconds you will be dead."

The German lifted his Spanish automatic high and levelled the barrel at Mark's head. From the corner of one eye Randall saw Irene scuffling her foot silently against the wheel of the chair she was tied into. A smile broke from the corner of von Jurgund's mouth and Randall could sense him beginning to squeeze the trigger.

Randall's eyes narrowed as he expected the end. Instead something caught him in the knees with a sharp clatter and he and the German went down in a writhing heap as Irene's wheelchair came spinning into them.

Randall landed on top of the German and grabbed his skinny neck with two hands as they struggled for the gun that had gone clattering across the floor. Irene in the wheelchair was in a heap in an opposite corner.

Mark pounded von Jurgund's head into the parquet flooring and made a dive for the glint of steel six feet away. The German, gasping for air was on top of him and digging his sharp nails into the skin beneath Randall's collar. Mark rolled with the monkey on his back and brought the barrel of the automatic crashing against the German's thin white face. As the blood ran from the cuts Randall grabbed the moaning killer and hefted him against the cabin wall. He lay there quietly, the blood smeared across his hair and face as Mark picked himself up and went to the girl in the toppled chair.

She was dazed from the fall and came awake with a murmur as Randall smoothed her copper-red hair softly. She looked up at him and Randall knew that the feelings he had in Berlin ten years ago were still very much alive.

(Continued on page 52)

NEW DISCOVERY IN HYPNOTISM

shows how to hypnotize in 30 seconds!

Yes, an amazing new method has been developed to bring on quick easy induction of the hypnotic trance. Now, for the first time, you too can benefit from this recent discovery in hypnotic induction.

Exclusively in
How to HYPNOTIZE
QUICK RESULTS

WANT TO HYPNOTIZE YOUR FRIENDS? YOUR CLUB MEMBERS? Here is a remarkable primer that shows you how to master entirely new methods that are not only sure-fire in their results but quick and easy to achieve. It is actually guaranteed to give you all the know-how necessary to induce the trance in others. The author, a widely experienced hypnotist, gives you the exact positions to take, the precise phraseology, and shows you step by step exactly how to bring on the hypnotic trance, how to deepen it, and how to terminate the trance swiftly and effectively without any dangers whatsoever.

USED BY DOCTORS
This amazing primer is being used by doctors and psychologists to learn hypnotic induction.

PHOTOGRAPHICALLY ILLUSTRATED
40 photographic how-to illustrations

ONLY $1.98

TRY 10 DAYS FREE

FREE 10-day examination of this book is offered to you if you mail us coupon today. If not delighted with results return it within 10 days for full refund of the purchase price.

GUARANTEE
This guarantees you that HOW TO HYPNOTIZE will show you how to induce the trance, or your purchase price will be refunded upon return of the book.
Signed BOND BOOK

BOND BOOK CO., Dept. H-221
43 W. 61st Street, New York 23, N.Y.

Send How To Hypnotize for 10-day free trial. My purchase price will be promptly refunded if I'm not satisfied.

☐ I enclose $1.98. Bond Book pays postage.
☐ Send C.O.D. I'll pay postman $1.98 plus postage.

NAME
ADDRESS
CITY   ZONE   STATE

RED MEANS BLOOD

"Anymore of them?" gasped Randall. "No just these four," said Irene. "They got me up here last night by calling for a manicurist. I fell for it. Can you imagine? I must be losing my touch." Randall took her arm and reached for the phone with his free hand. He told the ship's operator to get his home number and held on. Randall heard the phone ring once and then the click as it was picked up.

"Mr. Randall's residence," answered a cool voice at the other end. This time Mark recognized Nick Warden's voice right away.

"It's not every lawyer that has a full Brigadier for a houseboy," he said. "We're not taking any chances," chuckled Warden. "What happened?"

"We win the ballgame," said Mark "I've got two dead foul balls in the cabin and one more that might be but I haven't checked yet." Randall looked over at Irene and said, "I think we've got the pennant clinched too."

"Good work all around," said Warden. "The FBI will be aboard to look at the wreckage and there is an ambulance waiting for you two at dockside. Bring her here now."

"Okay Nick," said Randall.

Mark straightened out his inspector's uniform and looked over at Irene. "You keep that blanket around you and shield your face. We're going off in that wheelchair

BARKER-KARPIS GANG

(Continued from page 27)

were soon underway. Slinky gun-molls shared the gangsters bedrooms, despite Ma's jealous tirades. The boys needed relaxation and the girls provided it.

Then, on January 17, 1934, the gang pulled their biggest deal of their career. Kidnapping Edward G. Bremer, president of St. Paul's Commercial Bank, he was taken to Illinois and held there for three weeks. The kidnapping aroused the nation. Upon receiving payment of $200,000 in ransom the

---

• Private Eye

Irene nodded silently and Randall opened the doors of the suite and wheeled the chair out onto the deck and down the gangway as knots of passengers stepped aside to let the "invalid" pass.

They rolled down the ramp into the pier shed where a private ambulance was waiting. As they got into the gleaming white wagon, Randall spotted the FBI men going aboard. The ambulance started with a low whine of its siren and picked its way across the pier and out into the glare of harborfront morning light.

Irene looked up at him from the ambulance bed and said, "Mark, you know why I came back don't you?"

Mark nodded but she went on.

"Ten years ago I was a wild war starved kid looking for adventure but I never forgot the things you told about the reds Mark. They were all true and I've been trying to get out for years.

"Shh," said Randall. "We'll have plenty of time to talk about that after everything is cleaned up." He smiled, bent down and kissed her gently and murmured, "plenty of time... plenty."

THE END

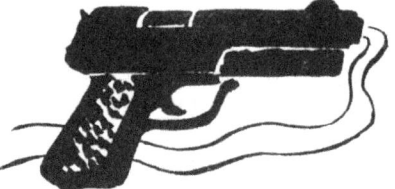

gang released Bremer in Rochester, Minn. This was what the F.B.I. had been waiting for. Kidnaping came under their jurisdiction and they moved in on the case.

SPECIAL AGENT WALTER FERRIS and a hand-picked group of investigators were given the difficult task of tracking the kidnappers down.

Their first clue was a fingerprint. When Bremer was taken from Bensen-

(Continued on page 54)

ROYAL JELLY, the Queen Bee's Special Food...ITS SECRET OF PROLONGED LIFE!

50 MILLIGRAMS OF PURE NATURAL ROYAL JELLY
complete 30 day supply
JENASOL FORMULA
$3.00 REG $7.50 VALUE

These are the 35 ingredients in every Jenasol Capsule:
COMPARE... FOR POTENCY, PURITY & PRICE!

ROYAL JELLY 50 Mgm.		Calcium	65 Mgm.
Choline		Phosphorus	50 Mgm.
Bi-tartrate	35 Mgm.	Rutin	5 Mgm.
Inositol	15 Mgm.	Vitamin B	2 Mcg.
dl-Methionine	10 Mgm.	Iron	3 Mgm.
Glutamic Acid	5 Mgm.	Liver, Desic.	5 Mgm.
Lemon Bioflavinoid		Potassium	5 Mgm.
Complex	5 Mgm.	Fluorine	50 Mcg.
Vitamin A		Copper	100 Mcg.
12,500 USP units		Molybdenum	100 Mcg.
Vitamin D		Zinc	100 Mcg.
1,000 USP Units		Cobalt	250 Mcg.
Vitamin C	75 Mgm.	Yeast	
Vitamin B1	10 Mgm.	Hydrolysate	10 Mgm.
Vitamin B2	5 Mgm.	Biotin	5 Mcg.
Vitamin B6	0.5 Mgm.	Iodine	0.5 Mgm.
Vitamin E	1 I.U.	Soya Bean	
Niacinamide	40 Mgm.	Lecithin	25 Mgm.
Calcium		Wheat Germ Oil	5 Mgm.
Pantothenate	4 Mgm.	Magnesium	3 Mgm.
Folic Acid	0.5 Mgm.	Manganese	0.1 Mgm.

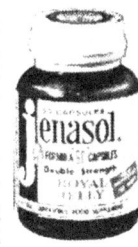

Doctors Report "Miracle" Royal Jelly May Change Your Whole Life!

How would you like to awaken one morning and find yourself possessed with a marvelous sense of "well-being," full of New Pep and Vitality? Wouldn't it be wonderful if you could feel increased vigor and enjoy a "new lease on life?" Now... Scientists say this may happen to you!

Royal Jelly May Mean "New Life" After 40

Reports from Europe tell of an 80 year old Gentleman whose physical condition would make a 50 year old envious. The man regularly partakes of Royal Jelly. According to a book published in England, when Russian Officials sent questionnaires to all the Centenarians (people over 100 years old) in the Soviet Union, more than half of them turned out to be beekeepers.

From France and Germany come amazing Scientific Reports of outstanding results obtained with Royal Jelly. One French Authority writes of women over 40 feeling increased sexual vitality and of a wonderful feeling of "youth and well-being" that resulted from continued use of Royal Jelly.

At this moment, in Leading Universities, Scientists and Nutritionists and Medical Doctors are doing extensive work to determine the exact role that Royal Jelly may play in Your Sex Life, Your Health and Your Emotional Health. These researchers are especially interested in its effects on those who have passed middle age. They are working on Royal Jelly because this rare NATURAL FOOD has been indicated to contain remarkable Energy and Sex Factors.

Doctor Paul Niehans, famous Swiss Surgeon and experimenter with Hormones says: "ROYAL JELLY is an activator of the glands"... Dr. Niehans discovered that many minor disabilities which bother millions of people such as tiredness, irritability, headaches, insomnia, physical and spiritual convulsions, were easy to treat with the Cellular Theraputics of the Secretion of the bees which we call Royal Jelly.

See How JENASOL Capsules May Help You!

Swallow one CONCENTRATED JENASOL RJ FORMULA 50 capsule daily. They combine 35 vitamins and minerals as well as the miracle food of the Queen Bee. This capsule dissolves instantly, releasing the super forces of Royal Jelly which go to work immediately and reenforce and healthfully strengthens your own natural functions which may have become deficient.

TRANQUILITY AND BLESSED RELIEF MAY AWAIT THE ROYAL JELLY USER

Here Are Some of the Symptoms of Approaching Old Age which Make Men and Women over 35 feel devitalized and "played out" before their time: PHYSICALLY, MENTALLY and EMOTIONALLY • "Human Dynamos" slow down • Dizziness • Weak feeling • Vague aches and pains • Listless, "don't care attitude" • Lacks recuperating power • Fatigues easily • Fails to get rest from sleep • Sexual weakness • Loss of mental efficiency and ability • Unable to make simple decisions • Can't concentrate • Nervousness • Tense feeling • Moodiness • Lack of emotional control • Loss of interest in work • Loss of self-confidence • Feeling of futility • Worries needlessly • Fear of future • Insecurity • Failing memory • No zest for life • Difficult to get along with • Embarrassed

Now You May Benefit from ROYAL JELLY... the "ELIXIR of YOUTH" of the Queen Bee

Two years ago, the world-famous French Nutrition Expert, Bernard Desouches, wrote a book praising Royal Jelly as a Life Prolonger and Extraordinary Stimulator of Sexual Virility of the Queen Bee.

The Best Laboratories of Europe gave the Doctors of the 2nd International Congress of Biogenetics a great surprise when they confessed that their famous Medical Cream for the skin was prepared with Royal Jelly. The Doctors all knew that with this cream sagging breasts were raised and mamary glands of women were activated.

ROYAL JELLY Wins Approval Before Congress* of 5,000 Doctors

The men of Medical Science who have experimented with Royal Jelly, claim that Royal Jelly will perform the function of INCREASING MEN & WOMEN'S WANING POWERS.

Jenasol R. J. Formula 50, in the opinion of these reputable physicians removes any possible danger for the layman in the use of these powerful, concentrated nutrional extracts. This is the latest and possibly the greatest advance in the history of Medical Science. This combination, created under the strict supervision of a Registered, Licensed Pharmacist, and Medical Doctor, named "Jenasol R. J. Formula 50," makes the use of these amazing elements perfectly safe.

Every man and woman who feels "old" and "played out" before their time should seriously consider the use of "Jenasol R. J. Formula 50" to increase their pep and energy.

Dr. De Pomiade, 80-year-old French Scientist and the Senior among the Physicians and Biochemists attending the Congress, said the Bee Secretion might have been known to Ancient Indians, Greeks and Romans, and might have been the "food for the Gods" or "Nektar" mentioned in the Mythology of these Countries.

Royal Jelly Reported to Help Those Suffering From:

Mental Depression... Loss of Appetite... Sexual Weakness... Digestive Disturbances Headaches... Decreased Vigor... Nervousness... Aches and Pains... Irritability.

Take "JENASOL Formula 50 Capsules" Entirely on Approval!

We feel sure that JENASOL may be the blessing you have been seeking, that we offer it to you on a complete NO RISK, Money Back Guarantee. Take one JENASOL CAPSULE each day. Then if you are not completely satisfied they have helped you to feel younger, to enjoy sounder sleep, to have a calmer disposition, and to lead a fuller, more enjoyable life, your money will be refunded, promptly and without question. Simply return the empty bottle and your JENASOL CAPSULES have cost you nothing. What could be fairer? You try JENASOL at our expense, and you are the only judge of their effectiveness. You must be thrilled with the wonderful results. BUT THIS OFFER IS NECESSARILY LIMITED as the supply of Royal Jelly is, each day, in GREATER DEMAND (ROYAL JELLY is a completely NATURAL PRODUCT, hence only limited quantities can be allocated to JENASOL.)

Don't delay... Get started immediately using this "MIRACLE" NATURAL FOOD that may help you feel good again... that may lead you to enjoy a new "lease on life."

Offices in Canada, Germany, Hawaii, Puerto Rico, Haiti, Cuba, Japan.

DOCTORS: Write on your letterhead for Clinical Samples

Observations by Doctors of the Medical Congress Who Took Royal Jelly and Observed its Use Directly

• Royal Jelly alleviates suffering of men and women in their critical years in a sensational manner.
• Royal Jelly acts on weakened, tired, eyes, giving instantly a sensation of new light.
• Feeling of tiredness disappears immediately.

• Royal Jelly gives a feeling of increased sexual drive and energy, especially to men and women over 40.
• Glandular studies may lead to new hope for men and women.
• Royal Jelly produces a pleasing state of relaxed well-being and eases tension.

DISCOVERER OF INSULIN
Dr. Frederick Banting

"The most complete Scientific Report on Royal Jelly was prepared under the direction of Dr. Frederick Banting.

"TEXAS A & M COLLEGE has been conducting experiments on Royal Jelly..."

"PROFESSOR G. F. TOWNSEND of ONTARIO AGRICULTURAL COLLEGE is resuming research on Royal Jelly..."

Life May Begin Again After 40 as Queen Bee's Natural Food Rebuilds Man's Vitality and Drive

Royal Jelly is totally unlike honey, and has baffled scientists since the 1700's. In 1894, some of the mystery was dispelled when Leonard Bordas, a French scientist, discovered that Royal Jelly is secreted by special glands located in the heads of worker bees whose job is to nurse the Queen.

Intrigued by the strange longevity and extraordinary sexual powers of the Queen Bee, leading scientists have been trying to discover the Secret Factor in Royal Jelly that so benefits the Queen Bee.

It is not surprising that Royal Jelly has attracted Medical Attention throughout the world... Here is the substance, the sole diet of the Queen Bee in which lies the secret of the difference between her and the rest of the hive. For the Queen lives to 6 years, whereas the 20 to 40 thousand worker bees and the few hundred drones live but a few short months. The Queen Bee larva looks like all the rest, including all of the female worker bees. But only SHE is fertile, producing some 400,000 eggs annually.

Her food is ROYAL JELLY, secreted from the glands of the worker bees. The ingredients are nectar and pollen, plus honey, combined in a mysterious way by Nature to make up the "miracle food" ROYAL JELLY...

No Doctor's Prescription Necessary

Order ROYAL JELLY with complete confidence. If for any reason JENASOL fails to satisfy you, your money will be refunded in full. Try it at our expense!... JENASOL CO., World's Largest Producers of Royal Jelly Products... serving over a QUARTER A MILLION PEOPLE — in the U.S.A. and 45 foreign countries; 22 E. 17th St., Dept. MD-11 New York 3, N. Y.

Men and Women Agents Wanted. Write for Free Literature.

MAIL THIS COUPON TODAY!
YOU OWE IT TO YOURSELF TO TRY ROYAL JELLY!

JENASOL CO., DEPT MD-11   22 East 17th St., New York 3, N.Y.

☐ I enclose $3.00 cash, check or M.O. for full 30-day supply. Please send me the JENASOL RJ FORMULA "50" PLAN. Each JENASOL 50 MGM. ROYAL JELLY CAPSULE is fortified with 35 EXTRA VITAMINS, MINERALS, LIPOTROPIC and HEALTH GIVING NUTRITIONAL FACTORS making JENASOL AMERICA'S BEST FOOD SUPPLEMENT VALUE. I understand the very first capsules must help me to feel good, and I must be completely satisfied in every way with the results I get from JENASOL, or my full purchase price will be refunded promptly and without question. (I save up to 85¢ by sending payment with order; JENASOL ships postage paid.)

☐ Please send 30-Day Supply DOUBLE STRENGTH 100 MGM. ROYAL JELLY JENASOL CAPSULES (Twice the Royal Jelly), FORTIFIED with same, identical vitamin-mineral formula as JENASOL 50 MGM. CAPSULES. I enclose $5.00 cash, check or M.O.

Name ....

Address ....

City.................................Zone.....State....................

☐ Send C.O.D.; I will pay on delivery plus postage and C.O.D. Charges.

ALL ORDERS RUSHED IN PLAIN WRAPPER

*Private Eye

BARKER-KARPIS GANG

(Continued from page 52)

ville, Illinois, to Rochester, Minn., he recalled that his abductors had filled the gas tank from an emergency can which was later tossed out of the car. Alerting the communities between Bensenville and Rochester to be on the lookout for such a can, the G-men struck pay-dirt when a farmer turned up with it. In the F. B. I. laboratory a latent fingerprint, identified as that of Arthur Barker, was developed on the can.

Knowing they were now dealing with the Barker-Karpis Gang, the Agents intensified their search. Here was an opportunity to bring the vicious gang to bay, and the G-men warmed to their task.

In St. Paul, the F. B. I. Agents turned up a second clue. The four flashlights used by the gang to give the pay-off signal were found and traced. The salesgirl who sold them identified Karpis from a photograph as the man who purchased them. The chase was on.

As the pressure of pursuit mounted the gang used every possible means to elude capture. They even underwent plastic surgery, and Karpis had his fingers shaved almost to the bone in a futile effort to alter his fingerprints. These were desperate days indeed as one gang member after another fell into the F. B. I.'s tightening net.

There was the matter of Russell Gibson, one of the gang's younger members. Gibson was holed up in a Chicago apartment with his mistress when the F. B. I. closed in. Panicked, the girl cried out. She pleaded that Gibson surrender. Gibson's reaction was to snatch up his loaded rifle. Flinging open the door he fired away. In the ensuing battle, and despite the fact that Gibson wore a bullet-proof vest, the G-men aim was unerring. A well placed shot nailed the gangster and he fell dead on the landing.

Gibson's death added to the gang's jittery nerves. By the fall of '34 a dozen more of the gang had been picked up by the F. B. I. and three were killed when resisting arrest.

In Cleveland, Karpis, the two Barker boys, Fred and Arthur, and two of their hoods were staying in a hotel. Their girls were with them, including Karpis' mistress, shapely Dolores Delaney. Overwrought and tense, the girls had indulged in a drinking bout. One of them turned on a radio and tuned in a hot band. Liquored up, they kicked off their shoes, wriggled out of their clothes. One began to strip-tease. Stark naked, she was doing the burlesque version of the bump and the grind when the wail of sirens filled the night. The hotel desk had been flooded with complaints and the riot squad was on its way.

"The cops!" yelled one of the gangsters.

Sobered by fear, the girls scrambled into their clothes as the gangsters hustled them out. Leaving by the hotel's side entrance, they raced for their car as the police roared up. Karpis opened fire as the squad car screeched to a halt. Within seconds the police were returning the fire. Terrified bystanders screamed in terror as bullets whined and splattered against the sidewalk and the walls of buildings.

Still, despite the furious exchange laid down by the police, the gangsters and their molls managed to pile into their getaway car. A last burst filled the swaying vehicle with holes as it roared off into the night.

The narrow escape led to their splitting up.

"It's the best bet," Karpis announced. "Dolores and me are headin' for Cuba. You boys had better make tracks too."

Arthur Barker went off to Chicago. Ma and Fred headed south. Despite these maneuvers, the F. B. I. kept up a dogged pursuit. Luck came to them in Chicago when they nabbed Arthur Barker in his hideout.

"I don't know where Ma and Fred is," he protested when questioned.

Going through his pockets the agents found a map of Florida with a circle pencilled around the town of Ocala.

Special agents Walter Ferris and Dave McMorris along with 11 other selected investigators boarded a plane out of Chicago not long afterwards. Arriving in Ocala they began their investigation.

"Sure I know him," a local merchant remarked while pointing to a picture of Fred Barker. "His name is

* Private Eye

Blackburn. He and his mother have a real nice place out on Lake Weir."

A stake-out in the vicinity of the cottage positively identified the occupants as being Ma and Fred Barker.

In the pre-dawn light of January 17, 1935, the F. B. I. men closed in. Five agents were posted on the highway to deroute traffic. Seven others, led by Walter Ferris, crept forward and surrounded the silent, palm-shaded cottage.

When Ferris' first warning was ignored, the G-men slipped their guns off safety and braced themselves. When the burst of machine-gun fire from the cottage sent Ferris scurrying for cover, a withering fire was returned.

THE BATTLE RANGED for two hours. As machine-gun fire continued to come from an upstairs window, the G-men poured bullets and tear gas into every part of the house. At long last there was no responsive shooting from the cottage.

Moving forward cautiously the G-men entered the bullet-ridden building. In an upstairs bedroom lie the bodies of Ma and Fred Barker. Both were dead. Fred had been shot eleven times, Ma three. Ironically enough, they had died exactly one year to the day after the Bremer kidnaping. A year of pursuit had ended in an anniversary of death.

Alvin Karpis was captured in New Orleans some months later, and both he and Arthur Barker were sentenced to life imprisonment in *Alcatraz*. In January, 1939, Arthur Barker was killed while attempting to escape. Karpis continues to serve. Like others before them, the infamous Barker-Karpis Gang had come to its ignominious end.

* * *

Since members of the Federal Bureau of Investigation have always preferred anonimity for the better performance of their hazardous duties, it is in compliance with this preference that the actual names of the F. B. I. agents have not been used in this factual account.

DON'T MISS THE NEXT EXPLOSIVE ISSUE OF PRIVATE EYE WATCH FOR IT!!

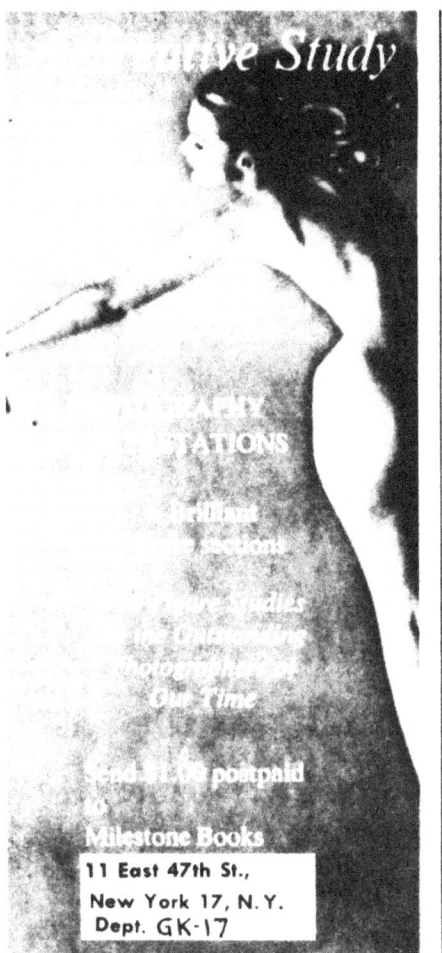

Send $1.00 postpaid to
Milestone Books
11 East 47th St.,
New York 17, N.Y.
Dept. GK-17

FEATURES
- Personalized With Your Initials
- It's Portable—Sets Up Indoors Or Out
- Built-in Shelf Holds Full Party Supplies
- Stain Resistant Bar Top

It's Big—39" wide, 38" high, 13" deep

Sturdily built of aluminum laminated and wood grain finished Multi Flute Fibreboard, this handsome personalized Home Bar is resistant to alcohol and soda stains. Handy built-in shelf holds full supply of bottles, glasses and napkins. Full size bar top holds drinks, pretzels, chips, etc. Sets up in a jiffy and folds compact for easy storage. A beauty for your home and a novel gift. State initials desired with each order

WORK
IN FOREIGN COUNTRIES
Write for OUR FREE foreign job reports.

Great opportunities in South America, Europe, Asia, Africa, Australia. Experience not necessary. *Higher pay.* Ages 18 to 50. Men and women. Want to work on a ship or yacht, traveling to islands and foreign countries around the world? Write for OUR **FREE** Ship and Yacht Job Reports. Experience not necessary. Higher pay for men and women. *Don't delay.* Write us today. Mail the coupon below for **FAST RESULTS.**

DAVENPORT FOREIGN SERVICE, Dept. 67
G.P.O. 1354, NEW YORK 1, N.Y.

Rush your **FREE** Foreign Job Reports and your **FREE** Ship and Yacht Job Reports.

Name_____

Street_____

City_____ Zone_____

State_____

PERSONALIZED HOME BAR

ONLY $5.98

*Personally Initialled
It's Portable
For Parties,
Gatherings
Basement*

This handsome portable Home Bar, personalized with your initials in a striking 3-dimensional contrast, makes it easy to serve guests in style. Made for both indoor and outdoor use. Its handsome contrast of wood grain and gold finish makes for a sparkling setting in the home. Adds class to any party or gathering, and points up the cleverness of its proud owner. And, for relaxing at home, in the parlor, den or basement it's certainly a convenient, handsome addition. Only $5.98. Comparable in satisfaction and utility to bars selling for $30. A perfect gift for any occasion.

10 DAY FREE TRIAL
Order today! If not delighted return for refund. Because of its large size we are forced to ask for 63¢ shipping charges

---

MONEY BACK GUARANTEE

S. J. Wegman Co., Dept. BR-16
LYNBROOK, NEW YORK

Rush my new personalized portable Home Bar at once. If I am not delighted I may return it after ten days Free Trial for prompt refund of full purchase price

☐ Send C.O.D. I will pay postman on delivery plus C.O.D. shipping charges
☐ I enclose $5.98 plus shipping charges

NAME

ADDRESS

MY INITIALS ARE

SING A SONG OF SEX-MAIL
(Continued from page 12)

OVID WAS HER MASTER
He Guided Her From the First Flirtation to the Ultimate Conquest

From him she learned the ancient mysteries of love, its unsuspected pleasures. Under his tutelage her dormant womanhood awakened and she became irresistible. Men broke down the doors in surrender to her will.

Ovid's ART OF LOVE is now available to those who are not afraid to try the unusual. Banned when first published and still hard to get in an untampered version, the book tells all in clear unashamed language. Everything is detailed from the first approach to the final conquest. It's as old as the oldest love ritual, newer than the newest sex book. Completely illustrated and beautifully bound.

ONLY $1.98

SEND NO MONEY... TRY 10 DAYS

BOND BOOK CO., Dept. AT-851
43 W. 61st St., New York 23, N. Y.

Please send Ovid's THE ART OF LOVE on 10-day free trial in plain wrapper. If not pleased, I get my purchase price refunded at once.

☐ I enclose $1.98. Send Postpaid.
☐ Send C.O.D. I'll pay postman $1.98 plus postage.

Name_____
Address_____
City_____ Zone___ State____
Canada and Foreign—No C.O.D.'s.
Send $2.50 with order.

Sassy Stories

THE QUEEN OF CAPER brings you old-time French favorites, long circulated by word of mouth. Some are true stories, frolics of the bigwigs, barely veiled. Some are sly, ingenious concoctions. Some are bold burlesque. All make bang-up, blowout entertainment, with ACTION louder than words.

Featuring: *Assault and Flattery, The Ghost in Nighties, The Masked Lady and the Frenchman, The Widow and the Spanish Horse, The Stable Boy and the Lady, Mutual Revenge, The Amorous Monkey,* and many other beauts!

In THE QUEEN OF CAPER you get the best of the *Heptameron* by Margaret, Queen of Navarre. It's adult reading — a sassy classic, long censored and still hard to get. Enjoy the untampered text, an exact translation of the famous French original. Enjoy the waggish, full-page pictures by a talented artist.

THE QUEEN OF CAPER is guaranteed to "sass up" your night life or your money back. Send $2 or pay postman cost plus postage.

PLAZA BOOK CO., DEPT. Q-1111
109 Broad St., New York 4, N. Y.

I climbed into my convertible and wheeled through the afternoon traffic to Annette Dahl's apartment. A 20-buck bill bought me a little information—but not much—from the doorman. The building superintendent cost another 20. That was for answers. I gave him a folded C-note when he told me Annette and the tenants of the apartment next to hers were all out.

"I'm a private," I grunted, flashing my buzzer. "I want to take a fast look around."

Annette's apartment was sexy—sexy as hell. I went through it fast and found nothing but a fortune in clothes and furs.

I also found the one-way glass mirror—right beside the bed, where it would reflect all the intimate details of the outings and games. The next-door apartment was deserted—and all the recording and photographic equipment had been cleaned out.

"When does the doll come back?" I asked the super.

"She usually comes in around six or seven—then, if her sugar-poppa don't show, she goes out and doesn't return until after midnight," he told me.

MY NEXT STOP was at the *Daily Express* office. Tad Hendry, the assistant city editor, was an old pal. He let me use the "morgue"—where the paper keeps its files and clippings on all the stories it has ever run. I dug into the envelope marked "Willoughby, J. Henderson."

I read through the clippings—society items mostly. Then, something in one of the gossip columns caught my eye. Karyn Willoughby had been seen at the Key Largo—the night club where Annette Dahl tried to make like a chanteuse.

It took me an hour to get out to her swank house in the upper-crust suburbs.

To my surprise, Karyn Willoughby opened the door herself. She must've been dressing to go out, for she was wearing a sheer robe—

"Your husband sent me," I lied to her.

Karyn Willoughby—5' 6" of lush and lovely female—stepped aside and nodded for me to come inside. She led me into a drawing room, asked me if I wanted a drink and, when I said I'd have Scotch, mixed two at the corner bar.

"Let's not fence," she murmured again. "I know who you are—and what you are. My husband had *my* private detective trailing him when he went to your office!"

"So?"

"So, drop my husband's case!" she snapped. "Forget the whole thing—and I'll make it worth your while!"

"Yeah?" I drawled "How?"

"With money—and with this," she said. She put her glass down and moved toward me. In a moment, she was in my arms and her hungry mouth burned against mine.

I felt the soft, perfumed curves. She was all over me—and I figured I might as well relax and enjoy whatever came next. An instant later the nymph jerked herself free, lashed out with her right hand and raked my map with her long, red nails.

"Get out," she smiled. "Now. If you're smart, you'll chuck the case over. And as I said, then you can come back."

I got. I climbed into my car. It was 6:30. I started back for town. I stopped off and made a phone call to Willoughby, had a couple of double Scotches and a bleeding steak—and went to a movie. I came out of the theater at 11:45 p.m.

ANNETTE DAHL LIVED in a huge apartment building. The doorman I'd greased had gone off duty and there

(Continued on page 58)

at last...a complete, modern guide to lasting mutual sexual happiness for all couples.

Illustrated SEX FACTS

By DR. A. WILLY, DR. L. VANDER, DR. O. FISHER AND OTHER AUTHORITIES

Available in this Country for the first time

THIS GIANT SIZE BOOK CONTAINS HUNDREDS OF AUTHENTIC, ENLIGHTENING ILLUSTRATIONS — *many in life-like color.*

Now available to the public in this country, for the first time, is this big guide to modern married sex practice. Written and illustrated by the most noted physicians and medical artists on sexual enlightenment. See and read how you can acquire enduring, harmonious married love by means of hundreds of exclusive, authentic pictures (many in true-to-life color), plus detailed step-by-step instructions written frankly and simply. This complete, large book includes important NEW information and illustrations never released here before. This book is a frank, straightforward presentation of facts to satisfy mature interest in the sex functions of the human male and female. Gives the most helpful authoritative guidance on sex problems of every kind — both abnormal as well as normal. Clearly understand and see the physiology and functions of the sex organs of both male and female. Many troubled men and women have found a new, happy married sex life and new confidence in themselves by reading "The Illustrated Encyclopedia of Sex." Sells for $5.00—but it is yours for the amazing low friend-winning price of only $2.98. This offer good for a limited time only. Mail coupon NOW!

SEND NO MONEY! FREE 10 DAY TRIAL COUPON

CADILLAC PUBLISHING CO., Dept. F-454
220 Fifth Avenue, New York 1, New York

Send me "The Illustrated Encyclopedia of Sex" in plain wrapper marked "personal." I will pay postman $2.98, plus postage on delivery (sells for $5.00). If not completely delighted within 10 days, I can return book and my money will be refunded. I am over 21.

NAME

ADDRESS

CITY   ZONE   STATE

☐ Check here if you wish to save postage, by enclosing with coupon only $2.98. Same Money-Back Guarantee!
(CANADIAN ORDERS $3.50. NO C.O.D.'s.)

PARTIAL LIST OF 61 BIG CHAPTERS EACH A "BOOK" IN ITSELF

- Techniques that bring complete gratification to the sex act for male and female
- What causes climax in women
- Blunders made by men in sex act. How to avoid them
- Technique of first sex act on bridal night
- Why woman fails to attain climax
- Husband and wife attaining mutual climax
- How male organs function in intercourse
- How female sex organs function in intercourse
- How sexual urge in woman differs from man
- Woman's perfect complete sexual satisfaction
- How to derive perfection in sexual act
- Reactions of man and woman during sexual relations compared
- The truth about sex vitamins that improve sexual powers
- Natural birth control
- New discoveries in birth control
- Woman's fertile days
- Causes of sex drive in women
- Female frigidity, its causes and cures
- Causes and cures for sexual impotence in men
- Abnormal sex organs and what can be done
- How to correct male's premature climax
- Delaying sex life's finish
- Male change of life and its effect
- Causes and treatment of male and female sterility
- Feminine self-satisfaction
- Causes of sexual urge in men
- How sex activity affects weight of male and female
- How to use preparatory love towards greater satisfaction in sex act

Just a few of hundreds of frank, enlightening illustrated instructions!

PARTIAL LIST OF ILLUSTRATIONS WITH AUTHENTIC COLOR PICTURES!

- Male Sex Organs
- Showing functions of male sex organ
- Illustrating effects on breasts after pregnancy
- Showing areas of woman's organs producing highest sensations
- Watch step-by-step growth of child in pregnancy
- Complete Color Picture Story of Woman's Sex Organs
- Pictorial Story of Woman's "SAFE" days
- Picture Story of Cause of Sterility in women
- Cross Section of the Hymen in various stages
- Cross Section Showing Cause of Woman's sexual ills
- Picture Story of normal Sexuality in male
- Picture Story of Woman's Sensation Curve
- Picture Story of most important cause of impotence
- Two Inserts of Female Bodies showing how pregnancy takes place

...plus many more pictured instructions

SING A SONG OF SEX-MAIL (Continued from page 56)

was another in his place. I breezed past him, got into one of the self-service elevators and went up to Annette's floor. I listened carefully. There were no sounds from inside. I took out a passkey, opened the door and let myself in. It was dark—and I sat down in an overstuffed chair to wait for her to come home. The Key Largo Club closed at 2:00 a.m.

She opened the door, came in and switched on the lights. She was startled, frightened to find me sitting inside. Her gorgeous face grew pale—and with her flaming redhair, the effect was to make her even more strikingly beautiful.

"What do you want?" Annette whispered in terror.

"I want to give you a chance to get out of a nasty deal with a whole skin," I told the girl. "I want to save you five years—years that you'll be spending in the can if you don't cooperate."

"I—I didn't want to do it," she said—and began to sob. "They—they made me..."

"Yeah, I figured that," I said—and I let her cry for a few minutes.

"Johnny Fuori and Pete Nestor—they manage the club—made me do it," she wailed. "They said they'd kill me if I didn't help them and that—that bitch!"

"Got a drink in the house?" I inquired. Annette nodded. She told me where to find the bar. I poured two big ones—one for her and the other for myself. I made her drink hers and downed mine.

"Congratulate me," I grinned. Annette's eyes—red-rimmed and swollen—showed that she didn't know what the hell I was talking about.

"Why?" she wanted to know in a hoarse whisper.

"Because I figured it all out a lot sooner than I'd expected."

"Will—will I go to jail?" Annette begged. I shook my head.

"I doubt it," I said. "I doubt it very..."

I never finished the sentence. She reached up and took my hands. She drew me down to her. Her lips were parted, moist. They came for mine. I kissed her and she moaned softly.

"What—what is this—a payoff?" I growled.

"No—no, Adam," she whimpered. "But it's been so long—since I've been loved by anyone young and handsome. I—I hated it with Willoughby. He was sick, crazy."

I didn't say anything. I reached out—and turned off the light...

IT WAS ALMOST 6:00 A.M. when I left. Annette was sleeping peacefully in her big playground bed when I slipped out of the apartment and went downstairs to my car. I climbed in, kicked over the engine—and headed for Karyn Willoughby's.

I parked a block from her house, walked to the front door and wangled it open with another passkey. I took off my shoes and eased inside. I found the stairs, climbed them and went down a long hall, stopping in front of each door along it, listening until I heard breathing from behind the next to last door in the corridor.

I eased the door open. It squeaked. I cursed under my breath and shoved it wide, reaching for the .38 snuggled up under my armpit at the same time. I didn't move fast enough, though.

"Hold it, bastard!"

I froze. The voice was a man's—and it came from the chair near the bed. Also there were two people in the bed—Karyn Willoughby and a scrawny, greasy-haired little rat.

"Expecting me?" I asked.

"Wise punk!" Karyn's boy friend in the chair snarled. "I ought to..."

"Don't, Johnny, for God's sake!" Karyn yelped.

"Hell, he's a burglar—and so I shoot him..."

"Then the police will come—and my husband will find out. We won't get a penny!..."

That stopped Johnny Fuori from pulling the trigger. It also made him look towards the bed, threw him off balance—and gave me the one-in-a-thousand chance. I took the odds—and dived.

I landed on him and the force carried both of us on the bed—on top of Karyn. I felt her writhe under me—and I can't say that it was an unpleasant feeling, but I didn't have time to think any more about it. I hit Fuori in the mouth with my right fist—and I felt teeth snap and break. I grabbed the other guy's hand—the one with the knife in it—and twisted.

"Help!" It was Karyn screaming. We were all tangled on the bed. Fuori and Karyn were stark naked. It made things a little easier. I slugged Pete Nestor where no man should be slugged and then smashed his nose flat with the butt of the revolver that I took from Fuori.

He went out—ice cold. Karyn was trying to get out of the bed. I grabbed her, spun her around and slapped her twice across the face—hard.

"Get up!" I yelled at her.

"Adam—listen to me... I'll do anything..."

"Shut up!" I rasped. "There's only one thing you can do for me, you cheap little whore. You can tell me where they are—the pictures, the tapes, all of it..."

"No!" I hit her across the face—once, twice, three times.

She brought them all out of her wall-safe after that—all the negatives and the prints, all the tapes. I glanced at the glossy prints and swore.

"I can see why you left your husband," I told Karyn. "But why in the name of God did you have to go about things this way? Why did you and your punk boy-friend over there pull Annette into the deal?"

Karyn broke down. She broke down completely—and spilled her guts. It was an ugly, sordid story. Her husband never knew about her nymphomania or about the fact that she had what amounted almost to a fetichistic mania for tough guys, thughs and punks. Johnny Fuori and Pete Nestor were only the latest of a long string of greasy sneck-boys she'd played around with.

"I—I knew that if we ever got around to getting a divorce his lawyers would dig up all the facts," Karyn admitted. "Then, I knew he'd have me—and I wouldn't get a cent. I have no money of my own—and he has millions. Johnny, I and Pete thought that we could get plenty this way..."

"I figured something like that," I shrugged. "I read up on you and your husband. One columnist mentioned that your father had gone broke and committed suicide during the Crash. Several columns mentioned that you'd been hanging around Johnny Fuori's club—the Key Largo. So that left only two possibilities. Either you were in on it with Johnny, Pete and Annette as part of the setup—or you and the boys were together and Annette was being forced into playing decoy. I'm glad it's the last—I kind of like that redheaded kid..."

(Continued on page 60)

Only 80¢ for 50-ft. 8mm Home-Movies!

Choose all you want now—COLOR or B&W—Brand New Films!

8mm ENTERTAINMENT MOVIES
50-ft. B&W—$2 Values.... Only 80c
5 for only $4 postpaid

Why pay $2 or more for 50-ft. 8mm Movies when you can get the very best for only 80c?

Check all the films you want:
- 12 "AFRO-MOOD" Cuban Dancer
- 13 "RHUMBA AMALIA" Cuban
- 23 "SILK STOCKING MODEL"
- 30 Gwen Caldwell "GIRL WITH $1,000,000 LEGS"
- 46 "SEASHORE FROLICS"
- 49 "BEAUTY PARADE"
- 60 "LINGERIE MODEL"
- 62 Kalantan "DANCE NOCTURNE"
- 64 "WOMEN OF BALI"
- 68 Cleo Moore "MODELS STOCKINGS"
- 73 Cute "AIRPLANE MECHANIC"
- 77 "ARFO-CUBAN RHYTHMS"
- 82 Kalantan in "BUDDHA DANCE"
- 86 "GIRLS WRESTLING"
- 90 Barbara Nichols "MAMBO"
- 92 Dolores Del Raye "ST. LOUIS WOMAN"
- 94 "HINDU TASSEL HASSELL"
- 101 "CAUGHT IN BARBED WIRE"
- 102 Sheree North
- 107 "THE TRESPASSER"
- 108 Nora Knight "EXOTIC DANCER"
- 117 Sheree North "SUN DANCE"
- 123 Choendelle "FOLLIES STAR"
- 125 "TEXAS LIL DARLIN"
- 126 "THAT GAL FROM DALLAS"
- 127 Tempest Storm "DESERT DANCE"
- 129 Sheree North "WASTE BASKET BLUES"
- 131 Linda "THE SUNBATHER"
- 133 "UNDERWATER DANCE RHYTHMS"
- 135 "TURKISH DANCER"
- 149 Lian "EXOTIC PARISIAN"
- 168 Arlene
- 182 "EXOTIC SWAN DANCE"
- 185 "LOUISIANA STRUT DANCE"
- 187 Jerrima "SOUTH SEA BELLE"
- 193 Blaze Starr "DANCE OF FIRE"
- 198 "MAID'S DAY OFF"

100-ft. B&W "Dancers", $1.60 each
- IRISH McCALLAH No. 52
- CLEOPATRA, No. 70
- CANDY BARR, No. 115
- SHEREE NORTH Screen Test, No. 120
- LILI St. CYR "SALOME" No. 8
- KALATAN FIRE DANCE, No. 83
- NEJLA ATES, Turkish Dancer, No. 165

200-ft. B&W "Specials", $3.20 each
- Pie a la Mode, Cast of 6, No. 31
- Underwater Spearfishing, No. 69
- Italian Beauty Queens, No. 99

50-ft. B&W "Features", $1.00 each
- Sammy Lee Dives, Olympic Champ, No. 7
- Underwater Ballerina, No. 16
- Rhapsody on Ice, No. 11
- Acrobatic Waltz, Baton Twirler, No. 35

Most Beautiful Girls in the World

Famed MISS UNIVERSE contestants pose and parade for you. These lovelies were chosen from all over the world. Our cameras show them at their best.
- MISS UNIVERSE CONTEST, No. 50, 200-ft. B&W $3.20
- MISS UNIVERSE BEAUTY PARADE, No. 85, 100-ft. B&W $1.60

SATISFACTION GUARANTEED by Special Exchange Plan

Rush Coupon for Fresh New Subjects Direct-to-you from Hollywood

COLOR MOVIES OF ROSE PARADE
Only $5 for

50-ft. film of "High Spots" or full 200-ft. Complete Reel for $20

Movie Newsreels covered the full 1959 Pasadena New Year's Rose Parade with expert cameramen—shooting in glorious Kodachrome Full Color. Using "Zoom" lens they got intimate close-ups of glamorous beauty queens and flower-bedecked floats. Enjoy this famed parade at home. Guaranteed to delight you with color, clarity, finest quality optical color print—or money back.

- ☐ 50-ft. Color "High Spots" $5
- ☐ 200-ft. Complete Reel Color ... $20

OTHER FULL COLOR FILMS
50-ft. reels .... $5 each

Nature's Scenic Wonders in Kodachrome Color
- ☐ GRAND CANYON
- ☐ YELLOWSTONE
- ☐ YOSEMITE PARK
- ☐ SEQUOIS NAT'L PARK
- ☐ BOULDER DAM
- ☐ NIAGARA FALLS
- ☐ SANTA CLAUS LANE—Hollywood stars parade down Hllwd. Blvd. with elephants, camels, bands, etc.
- ☐ HAWAIIAN DANCERS—Natives show exotic talent against floral backgrounds, colorful beach scenes.
- ☐ ICE FOLLIES—Lavish skating production by top performers.
- ☐ DESERT FLOWERS—Fascinating color close-ups.

**MAIL COUPON NOW
GET FILMS BY RETURN MAIL**

Carnival of Color Exotic "MARDI GRAS"

"Anything goes" in gay New Orleans during the Mardi Gras festival. Dancing in the streets —fantastic costumes—unbelievable parades. See the masked revelers cavorting, in color.

- ☐ 100-ft. in COLOR .... only $10
- ☐ 100-ft. in B&W $3

DANCE ARTISTES—IN COLOR!
50-ft. .... $5 each
- ☐ KALANTAN
- ☐ JERRIMA
- ☐ LIA OF PARIS
- ☐ BLAZE STARR
- ☐ DELORES DEL RAYE
- ☐ BETTY HOWARD

FEATURE DANCERS—IN COLOR!
100-ft. .... $10 each
- ☐ LILI ST. CYR
- ☐ NEJLA ATES

50-ft. MICKEY MOUSE AND DONALD DUCK MOVIES, $2 each
- No. 1502A "MICKEY'S LUNCH BREAK"
- No. 1503A "MICKEY, THE GORILLA TAMER"
- No. 1504A "MICKEY'S QUICK EXIT"
- No. 1505 "MICKEY, THE CONGO KILLER"
- No. 1506A "MICKEY, THE NURSEMAID"
- No. 1507A "MICKEY'S BAD DREAM"
- No. 1508A "MICKEY AND LITTLE EVA"
- No. 1510A "MICKEY'S BAD NIGHT"
- No. 1511A "MICKEY'S ROYAL BATTLE"
- No. 1512 "MICKEY'S FOOTBALL MANGLE"

100-ft. MICKEY MOUSE and DONALD DUCK MOVIES, $3.50 each
- No. 1402B "MICKEY GETS HIRED AND FIRED"
- No. 1404B "MICKEY & THE MECHANICAL BOXER"
- No. 1405B "MICKEY'S WILD CRAZY DREAM"
- No. 1407B "MICKEY AND PRINCESS CHARMING"
- No. 1451B "DONALD'S SUPER SERVICE"
- No. 1452B "FAST AND FURIOUS DONALD"
- No. 1454B "DONALD'S DAY OFF"

100-ft. CHARLIE CHAPLIN Screen Classics, $3.50 each
- 254 "ROMANTIC CHARLIE"
- 255 "CHARLIE THE REPORTER"
- 256 "CHARLIE DOING HIS BEST"
- 257 "TWO LITTLE NEMOS"
- 258 "CHARLIE THE BONEHEAD"
- 259 "SIDE DOOR PULLMAN"

☐ **FREE CATALOG**—All kinds of movies— for Kid Shows—Adults

YOU DON'T NEED A PROJECTOR!

This new 8mm Movie Viewer enables you to see 50-ft. 8mm movies in fast or slow motion.

Only $5.95 postage-free.

Tear out this page and *Mail* to: **MOVIE NEWSREELS, Dept. 195
480 Lexington Ave., New York 17, N.Y.**

☐ Rush me 8mm Movies listed here—postage-free. I enclose $ _____ payment in full. You guarantee satisfaction or exchange plan.

☐ Rush me 8mm VIEWER for $5.95 postage-free.

YOUR NAME ....

YOUR ADDRESS ....

CITY .... ZONE ...... STATE ....

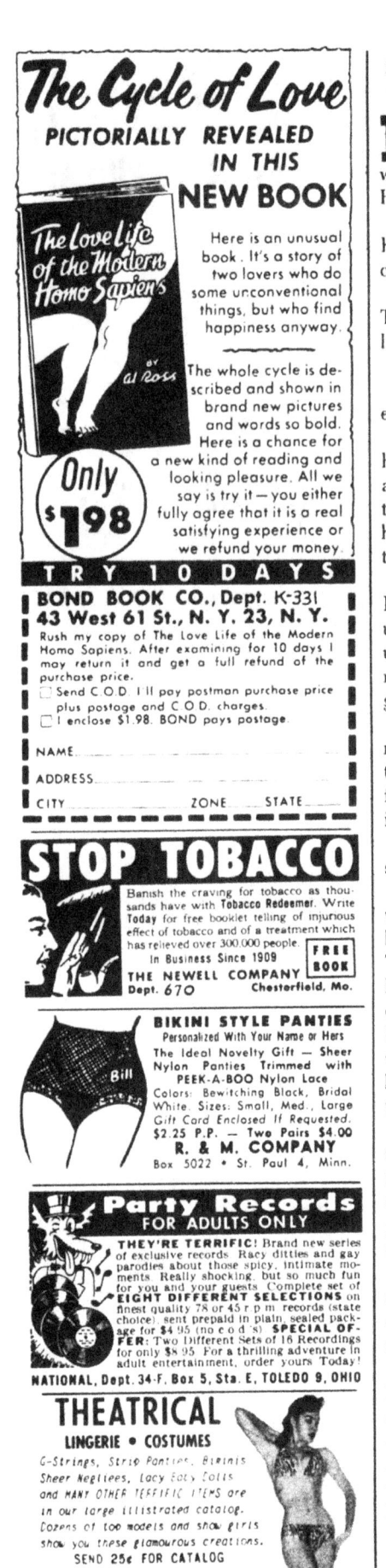

SING A SONG OF SEX-MAIL
(Continued from page 58)

I WAS TIRED—AND I FELT DIRTY. I went to my office and telephoned J. Henderson Willoughby.

"Come on up to my office," I told him. "I've got everything—and you can have it all for 25 Gees, $15,000..."

He began to yowl and splutter. They're all like that—save them a million and they'll argue about peanuts.

"You said $10,000!" he yelled.

"Okay, have it your way," I laughed. "Don't come around at all..."

He showed up, of course. I made him sit around until the banks opened and then we both went down and got the $15,000—in cash. Then I took him back to my office and handed over the photographs and the tapes.

"The extra $5,000 is for Annette," I told him. "That should tide her over until she can get herself straightened up and find another job. If you so much as go near her again, I'll be the guy you'll have to tangle with..."

"I never want to see her again!" he rasped. Then he wanted me to tell him the whole story—how and where I'd found the photographs and the recordings.

"That's my secret, Willoughby," I said. "It's none of your business..."

Hell, the way I looked at it, Karyn was no prize. She was a bitch, but her husband was a depraved s.o.b. There was no reason to give him any lever with which he could beat her out of the alimony he'd have to pay. Besides, to my way of thinking, that was something he and Karyn and their lawyers would have to fight out among themselves.

I watched Willoughby leave and then I had a stiff drink from the bottle in my desk drawer. I guzzled five, maybe six, fingers, tossed the empty jug into the wastebasket—and locked up the office.

Annette was still asleep when I showed up at her apartment. I punched the bell-button. She came to the door, sleepy and surprised.

I slipped inside, closed the door behind me. I gave her a fast rundown on what had happened, gave her the 5 Gees I'd gotten for her from Willoughby, and stood there grinning when she put her arms around me and kissed me.

I'll be damned if I didn't feel like a Boy Scout as I followed her back into her bedroom...

THE END

"I SMASHED THE VICE-PHOTO RACKET"

(Continued from page 32)

Bruno was a little man with a big drug habit and it clung to his back like a ten ton weight. It started to show now in the way his eyes were twitching, and in the yawns he couldn't stop. "Tom," he said to me in a desperate whisper. "You gotta get me somethin'. I need it bad. A sniff, or a goofball. Or H. H'll do it. Tom." His clawlike hand grabbed me. "You gotta..."

I separated each of his fingers off my arm. "I don't have to do anything, Bruno... Besides, it won't help. Not for you. These screws are going to put you in a little cell and lock the door and throw the key away.

"Please, you've got to help me. You can, Tom. You know them. They'll listen to you..."

"I have to trade them something, Bruno. There are two sides to a deal." His eyes grew wary as I went on. "There's only one thing you've got to trade and that's a contact. A way to the inside of the racket..."

He backed away and fear was written on his face in capital letters. "No... I ain't bringing no cops in. These boys I'm with play for keeps and somebody will get hurt. Then I'll wind up in the middle with a great, big, empty bag..."

"Easy," I soothed. "It's not the cops. It's me..."

Kluve thought a moment, then he shrugged. "And if I agree, you'll get me out of here?" he asked doubtfully.

I smiled at him. "Before you can show me the way in, I have to show you the way out, don't I?" All of which goes to show that my business is like politics. It isn't what you know so much as who you know that gets the job done.

THE DIRTY PICTURE ROUTINE, as anybody who's been around police work knows, is a simple racket, depending on speed, secrecy and threats to maintain its safety. Bruno explained how his particular group worked as we rode downtown in a cab after I'd arranged for his release from the cell-

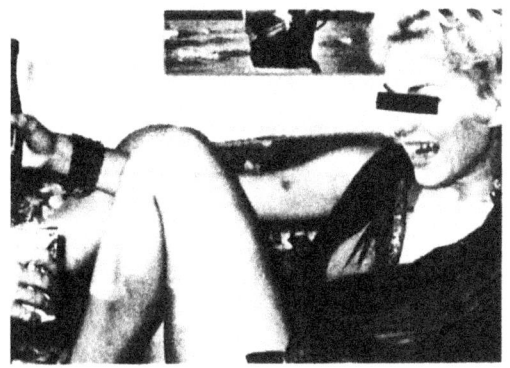

block. "The photo labs for the stills and the movies are hidden around town," he said. This was were the film was processed and printed. Then it was sent to a central warehouse for storage until it was shipped out. From here they serviced a five state area.

"Who's your boss?"

"You don't know him..."

"I know every punk with an illegal angle going in town..."

"Not him. He's new..." Bruno's contact with the big wheel was made through the Passion Pit, which was a strippers' cellar joint off Main. It was one of those smoky booze and broads spots where the tourists get taken down to their smallest change. Bruno and I walked down the steps and right away a readhead hit me in the chest with a pair of cleavages that looked like a crevasse in the Italian Alps. But I brushed her, and then a blonde who was ready to promise anything for a bottle of forty dollar champagne. I was looking for one of my own kids whom I used in my divorce setups, and finally spotted one. She was a dark haired, dynamic, little thing with a body that made many a man getting setup for a divorce raid ready to start his mistakes all over again in her bed. But the only language she understood was the one spoken by good, hard cash. I motioned and she came over. I bought her a drink and told the waiter to be sure he used the whiskey instead of the tea bottle. She was surprised and maybe a little complimented. Then I pointed a finger from her to Bruno. I told them I wanted the boss guy's name. They were scared and said that they didn't have it. They only knew of him as Georgie...

I insisted I wanted to talk to him. But they said he was too tough. They couldn't dare cross him. He'd chill them, maybe for good. I asked them who they were more afraid of, this Georgie or me. They didn't have to make the choice because just then the chippie got a sarcastic smirk on her lush lips. "Don't ask us," she said. "Ask Georgie. That's him coming down the stairs now..."

Through the smoke I looked toward the stairs. Georgie, hell! It was John Georgio, an oily haired young punk I'd seen in the morning lineup a couple of times. It was always on suspicion of strong arm stuff. I couldn't help but smile to myself as I realized that this was going to be no trouble.

The chippie wiped the smile from my face for she leaned over and let her long hair fall down so it touched my shoulders. I could smell the exotic perfume that was the mainstay of her profession and my eyes could look down her alpine crevasse until it touched bottom. "Don't be so happy, Tommy," she whispered. "Your work is just beginning. Georgie there ain't really Mister Wheel. He's just the contact for little cogs like Bruno and me..."

I walked over to the table. Georgio was lounging back, with his hand wandering up the inside of a floozie's skirt, and his legs spread out over a couple of chairs. He didn't hear me come up behind him. Not until I reached out, grabbed each of two chairs and yanked so that his legs came down with a crash and the hooker went flying off his lap with a squeal.

The punk came up angry and red-faced, with his hand going inside his jacket. But I slapped him down with a flathand chop right across the Adams Apple. The fight drained out of him like it was toothpaste coming out of a tube as he gagged and choked and tried to get his breath back. In the meantime, I had leaned over and relieved him of his hand-iron, a nasty little .32 on a .38 frame that he carried in a shoulder holster.

The waiters and the prostitutes and the B girls stood around staring open mouthed. Georgie came off the floor fighting mad. But I took it out of him again, this time with a clout across the bridge of his nose that almost separated it from the rest of his face.

He was down for good and I had to lift him up. The whole front of his shirt was red as if somebody had taken a brush and painted solidly from his chin to his belly. I dropped him into a chair and sat across the table from him. Wordlessly he stared at me with black eyes bright with fear.

His voice croaked "I know you, Nolan. You're an eye..."

"And I'll give you a black one unless you address me as Mister..."

"What do you want, Mister?"

"I told you. I want to buy a ticket through to the other end of the line..."

"Why?"

"I'm a photographer. I take dirty pictures..."

"You don't know one end of the camera from the other..."

"But I know one end of a gun from the other," I said hardvoiced and watched him flinch. I continued in the same tone. "Punk, I'm not sitting here to play twenty questions. The information I've got and the reason I want to see your boss is a little too heavy for you to carry around comfortably. Someday, somebody might start a little squeeze on me; the cops might ask too many questions. Then I'd have to go back and clean out all the odds and ends that knew about my connection with this, ah, operation. What would you rather be, an odd or an end?"

was to him as he went to phone. But I could watch him in the mirror and if he'd try anything I'd have turned around and shot him in the belly with his own gun. But he had been taught his lesson.

IN THREE MINUTES, Georgie was back. "They're gonna pick us up," he said through a handkerchief he held to his nose to stop the flood of blood. "Out front. In ten minutes..."

Exactly ten minutes later we stood out front on the foggy street when a big, black car pulled up. Two beefy, professional acting muscle men stepped out. They knew their business and in a second I was inside the car with one of them on either side of me. They took my own gun but I didn't tip them off that I had slipped Georgie's hand-iron into my pants and that it hung suspended next to my private parts. They handed me dark glasses that were completely opaque and even the sides were covered.

We purred along for a while, then pulled off the street and went into a driveway. There was the clang of a door and the car stopped. I was led out. They told me not to take off the glasses yet. A hand on my elbow led me across a thick rug. I heard women's voices. Then a man said I could take off the covers. I was in a large, luxuriantly decorated room with thick brocades on the windows and silk covers on the divans. Most luxurious

(Continued on page 62)

"I SMASHED THE VICE-PHOTO RACKET"

of all though, were the women. There were six of them, each selected for long curving legs and tight little waists; for sharp, jutting breasts, and long, luxuriant hair. I could see exactly what they had been selected for. Not one of them wore clothing. The girls were giggling and taking different poses and playing circus. Then I saw why. There were men there. Most of them middle aged, bald headed, with cameras resting on their paunches.

The punk Georgio came across and thrust a camera at me. "Here," he sneered. "You wanna take pictures..." The bleeding had stopped but his nose was sore and red looking. The camera he gave me was a complicated one but I pretended I knew what I was doing and shot pictures, from every conceivable angle, of the girls doing things in broadly suggestive nude poses.

Finally the photo session seemed to be over and the middle aged slobs reluctantly slipped out of the room under instructions from one of the beef boys. I acted as though I would follow but they blocked the door. So I turned back.

And then somewhere in the house we heard a door open. There was a loud buzzer. On one wall a red light started to blink on and off.

"Come on," Georgio said, touching his tender nose and looking at me like he was going to get even. "You wanna meet the Wheel? Well, he's in now..."

I wasn't so sure but I didn't have a chance to argue. The two beef boys grabbed my arms and hustled me through the doorway behind Georgio. We went quickly through a long, dimly lighted hall. Then a door was opened, the three of them stood outside and I was pushed, right into a black, stygian gloom, as the door slammed behind me.

I was still blinking when a voice said in a hissing whisper. "So you made it this far, Mister Nolan. I was afraid you might..."

The voice had a strange, haunting familiarity. I listened, trying to pin it down. My eyes were getting accustomed to the gloom and I could make out the shapes and forms in the room.

"You were foolish," the voice continued. "You were looking for something to get us on and so you came here and you took pictures of the naked girls. But that wasn't why you came... was it?"

I looked into the gloom and I could not locate where he was as I answered, "No, it wasn't. I've got a plan. Big distribution, big contacts. The perfect front for your operation. A detective agency. You can distribute all over. Nobody would suspect."

The voice cut me off with a chuckle. "A good try, Nolan. Very good, very ingenious. But we know about you. We know what you do, who you see. One of our big fears was that someone would set you on our trail. Tonight, someone did. So you're here. It won't do you any good though. You can't do anything against us because you're in this. Right along with the worst of us. You're an accomplice, Mister Nolan. In fact, if anyone ever checks you're one of the leaders in our group ...We have proof..."

Suddenly the darkness was split by a beam of light. The light hit the far wall and showed a picture in black and white. I was on the wall up there, leaning over naked girls and taking shots. The picture had been taken a little while before when I was in the other room.

"You see, Mister Nolan," the voice continued, "One picture is worth a thousand words. So you go home and forget about us. Otherwise we shall send prints of this and others like it to the police, the Obscenity League, the newspapers. You'll be ruined in this town. They'll hang you so high you'll be used as a sundial..."

I was silent a moment, thinking. That voice. I knew it. Knew it well. I was sure of it. And then it came to me. So simple. So beautifully easy. I laughed.

"This is no laughing matter, Mister Nolan."

"Oh, drop the noise. You can see me, so you know me. I can't see you, but I know you. Now I know your whole operation."

That voice sounded sad. "I'm sorry, Tom Nolan. I really am. I liked you, a hell of a lot. This is the way it'll have to be now. It's too big an operation to have you kick it over. Too much at stake, too well organized..." As he spoke a hand came into the light and it held a gun. The knuckles were whitening in a squeezing grip.

Not until then did I shoot him with Georgio's gun. I aimed for the thickest part of the body. A bullet going in there has to hit good. He choked, and his hand clenched: the gun went off aiming at the ceiling.

At the sound of the shots the door burst open and Georgio came bursting in, flipping on the lights and waving a gun in his hand. At the sight of the weapon I held he stopped still and shrivelled and dropped his gun. I waved him to one side and waited. Sure enough, the other two came running in, one at a time.

They came in tough and waving their weapons until they saw my gun and the body on the floor. Then their resolution ran out.

I called a private number I'd been given. When it was answered I said, "Come on over. It's finished. The Wheel is dead, and I've got three little cogs waiting for someone to pick them up."

IN FIVE MINUTES the police were there. A prowl car hit first. They relieved me of my prisoners. Then I walked over to the dead man. It was a real shocker. To think that this man, who meant so much to law enforcement in this town was actually the big wheel behind the lucrative obscene literature racket. I couldn't get over it.

I said as much to Captain Pat Monohan when he arrived. He turned the body over and shook his head. "Chewett... the head of the Committee Against Obscenity. No wonder none of our boys could get inside the racket.

I flipped on the film projector and the picture appeared on the wall showing me taking pictures of naked girls. "He thought he had me with this. It was supposedly proof that I was in the gang..."

The prints and the movie films were stored right there in the same building with the offices of the Committee Against Obscenity. Chewett had used the old adage. If you can't beat 'em, join 'em. Only he'd actually taken over. Except for me. There he'd stubbed his toe. Because he didn't know I had one requisite every successful cop needs—luck.

I proved it again later that night when I got home..... The light came on. The dark haired girl from the bar, the well built one, smiled at me when I asked what she was doing in my bed. "You bought me a drink," she said. "And I didn't pay you for it." Then she lifted the sheet and I could see her gloriously naked figure. "Come on, Tommy," she said in a husky voice. "Collect..."

THE END

BOSOMS and BULLETS

(Continued from page 49)

As I looked around me at the stuffed shirts, I began to feel more out of place.

We got off on the ninth floor and were met by a butler, and a few more friends of mine in blue.

"Your cards please."

The gals gave him the invites and went inside. I was to wait in the corridor with the officers of the law.

I could hear the ah's and oh's and knew that my two beautiful *señoritas* were going over with no strain. I settled back in my chair and began to think this whole thing over. As the evening wore on, my brain began to click. I went to the wall phone and asked to speak to my buddy Cy.

It was just about midnight, and the party sounded like it was first beginning, when Violet and Maria came out lugging their model cases.

"Sam darling you're such a strong sight to our eyes. Shall we go? We really must rush in order to make our plane at one o'clock." "Violet is right Sam. Why don't you say goodnight to your policemen friends and escort us to the airport."

I SAID MY GOODBYES to the boys, took the girls down on the elevator, waved to Cy on the way out of the lobby and hailed a cab.

As we approached the lonely road leading to the airport, I turned to look out the back window. My suspicions were confirmed.

"Your boy friends are back." Violet began to shake, but it was Maria who spoke up as her hands tightened on the strap of the models bag. "Sam, if those men should start trouble, I would like to offer you an incentive of five hundred extra dollars to get rid of them."

Before I had a chance to answer, they cut in front of the cab, and forced us off the road. Two men got out, guns blazing as I answered their fire. The cabbie ducked under the dash and I shoved the girls out the other door. I got out myself, and as I dashed to cover behind the front fender, I noticed one of the boys had a bandage around his neck. I must have grazed him in our battle in the alley earlier.

They weren't kidding around. They wanted these gals real bad. One of them started running forward, his gun spitting flame. He got off a last shot as he pitched over with one of my slugs in his middle. I took a fast look. It was the guy with the bandage on his neck. I crawled closer, and could see that he was also a Latin.

The shooting from the other hood stopped. I held my fire, and after a few minutes . . .

"*Señor*, just throw me the models bags, and I will go. No more shooting."

"How about the murder the girls saw committed? Don't you want to shut them up about that?"

"*Señor*, the only murder they might have seen committed was the one just now when you shot my unfortunate friend lying in front of you."

I realized then how close I had come to making a fool of myself. If I hadn't thought it over sensibly in the corridor of the hotel, I might have been forced to turn in my badge. Or had it taken from me.

I cupped my hand to my mouth.

"Look, I know the whole deal now. Those girls have been carrying jewelry which they have been stealing from all those shindigs they've been going to. You set them up, and they pulled the old double cross by hiring me. That way, no split. You find out, and with the aid of your dead slob gave me a good going over in their room. The only time they didn't lie to me is when they told me their screams scared you off. They also figured with me as escort, my police friends wouldn't even bother to search the model cases. They also knew I have friends in customs. That bit about looking me up in the phone book was baloney. They checked pretty carefully before they picked me as the patsy, right Violet and Maria?"

I turned around to where the girls were and stared into two neat little automatics. Both pointing at my beard.

Violet and Maria walked slowly around me. Violet made our cab driver come out, and then she yelled to the other character. "Pedro, let's forget about what's happened. We will make a deal, we shall split one third with you if you drive us safely away."

Whether he meant it or not, the creep accepted the offer in a hurry. They got into his car, and took off in the direction of the airport.

The cabbie still sweating bullets came over to me.

We got into the cab, and I told him to drive to the airport. On the way there, I told the driver how I figured the whole thing out, and then spoke it over with my buddy Cy. Cy was an efficient cop. By now the two chickies and their on again off again pal were in custoday at the hangar. I took a look out the back and those headlights were sure to be Cy and a few officers. When we arrived, I saw that I was right on both counts.

A S THE THREE WERE being led away, I offered a goodbye kiss to my ex clients, but they didn't seem to go for my little joke.

"Cy, let me ask you something. Those thefts were reported to the police and the insurance companies. How come they weren't made public?"

"It was very ticklish Sam. It meant questioning some very important and distinguished guests. It was reported all right, but requested to be handled under cover. I would say you're in line for a pretty good reward."

I sucked in some of that beautiful night air, and walked back to the squad car with Cy.

"In anticipation of that reward you were speaking about Cy, suppose we stop off some place, and I'll buy you a meal."

"I accept Sam. And you know what? I can sure go for a good Spanish meal. The kind they serve in that little place in your neighborhood."

I settled back in the seat and smiled. Cy could be a joker when he wanted to. I had enough Spanish dishes for awhile. I directed my next remark to officer O'Rourke who was driving.

"Drop us off at Chin Wong's."

Maybe it was the hour, or maybe the excitement, but I looked at Cy, and he looked at me, and we both started to laugh like hell.

THE END

IN ONE SPLIT SECOND

SICKNESS or ACCIDENT May Rob Your Savings!
Take Your Home! Split Your Family! Wreck Your Future!

PROTECT YOURSELF AND YOUR FAMILY WITH DEPENDABLE...

NATIONAL PROTECTIVE SICKNESS & ACCIDENT INSURANCE

ONLY 10¢ — Pays in Full the First Month's Premium For this Sickness and Accident Policy.

Don't wait until trouble strikes! In one split second, sickness and accident may hit you and, if you're un-insured, the enormous costs of hospital or home confinement, medicines and doctors bills may rob you of every cent you have! The National Protective Sickness and Accident policy is specially designed to help protect you against such misfortune. Only 10c puts your policy in force for the first 30 days—only $1.00 a month keeps it in force thereafter. Here, indeed, is Sickness and Accident insurance all America can afford.

Could You Use $100.00 a month?
Could Your Family Use $5000.00?

Here are just a few of the protection features of the great National Protective Sickness and Accident Policy...

PAYS $100.00 Per MONTH if disabled by accident payable from the very first day of medical attention at the rate of $25.00 per week for a maximum of 10 weeks if caused by a great many specified accidents such as while travelling on trains or in private automobiles or as a pedestrian.

Pays $71 to $100 per MONTH if laid up by specified sickness, originating 30 days after issue of policy. Payable from the first day of medical attention when disabled and house confined at the rate of $30.00 per month for the first week, at the rate of $60.00 per month for the second week and at the rate of $100.00 per month for the remaining period up to eight weeks.

PAYS $5000.00 ACCUMULATING TO $7500.00

for travel accidental loss of life, hands, feet or eyes. These benefits are payable for accidental death resulting within 30 days from date of accident or accidents occurring when riding as a fare-paying passenger on a train, bus, subway or steamboat and involved in the wrecking of such common carrier. All travel accident benefits for loss of life, sight or limbs automatically increases 10% a year for 5 years. Thus the $5000 benefit increases each year so that after the 5th year the benefit has risen to 50% or more, or a total of $7500.00.

NO MEDICAL EXAMINATION — NON CANCELLABLE
NO SALESMAN WILL CALL

National Protective Sickness and Accident Insurance is great insurance. No medical examination is required. In accordance with standard claim procedure the company reserves the right to determine the existence of good physical and mental health at the time of issuance of insurance as a prerequisite to payment of benefits. The company cannot cancel your insurance; it stays in force as long as prompt premium payments are made. If, however, for any reason you may desire to return the policy anytime within the first 30 days from in-force date, your 10c will be refunded.

NATIONAL PROTECTIVE LIFE INSURANCE COMPANY
Dept. 200   HAMMOND, INDIANA

Application
FOR ACCIDENT & SICKNESS POLICY

I am enclosing 10c. Please issue to me your $1.00-A-Month-Accident-and-Sickness-Policy based upon the statements I am giving you herein. If I am not entirely satisfied I will return the policy and you will refund my money. ISSUED TO PERSONS 15 to 69 YEARS—(GUARANTEED NON-CANCELLABLE).

Send Only 10¢ WITH THIS APPLICATION Pays in full the first month's premium for the policy. Thereafter rate is only $1.00 a month.

NATIONAL PROTECTIVE LIFE INSURANCE COMPANY
Dept. 200   Hammond, Indiana   IBM920
(Please use ink)

1. Full Name..
   (please print)   Given Name   Last Name
2. Home Address { Street and Number.............
   City.................................. Zone...........
   County.................................. State...........
3. Age.......... Date and year of Birth............
   Occupation...............................
   Height.......... Weight.......... Sex..........
4. Name of Beneficiary.............................
   Person to whom Benefit is to be paid in event of death
   Relationship...............................
5. Have you had medical advice or treatment or suffered from any accident or illness during the last five years?..........
   If yes, when and for what?..........
6. Are you now in good health, mentally and physically?..........
7. Do you have any physical defect or deformity?..........
8. Have you been injured while driving an automobile?..........
   If so, to what extent..........
   Signed at City.......... State..........
   this.......... day of.........., 19......
   The answers to the above questions are given to the best of my knowledge and belief.

Sign here..........   Policy 6022

Are You Giving Your Wife The Companionship She Craves?

YOU may be giving your wife all the love and care you are able to. You may have given her a good home, security, many of the conveniences all women yearn for. But is she completely satisfied? Are you giving her what she most expected on the day that you married her? *Are you giving her the full companionship of the man she loves?*

Or are you always "too tired" at the end of a day's work? Do you come home from work with only the "leftovers" of your energy for your wife and family? Is time catching up with you *too fast*... at work, at play?

If so, your condition may simply be due to an easily corrected vitamin and mineral deficiency in your diet. You owe it to yourself, if you are otherwise normally healthy, to find out whether a high-potency nutritional supplement such as VITASAFE capsules can help increase your pep and energy. And you can find out at *absolutely no cost* by taking advantage of this sensational no-risk offer!

25¢ just to help cover shipping expenses of this
FREE 30 DAYS SUPPLY HIGH POTENCY CAPSULES
LIPOTROPIC FACTORS, MINERALS and VITAMINS

Safe Nutritional Formula Containing 27 Proven Ingredients: Glutamic Acid, Choline, Inositol, Methionine, Citrus Bioflavonoid, 11 Vitamins (Including Blood-Building B-12 and Folic Acid) Plus 11 Minerals

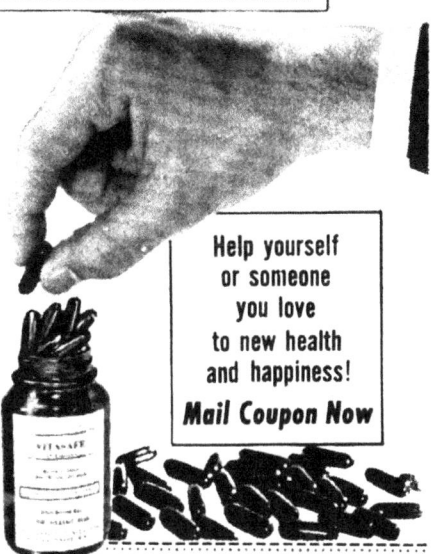

MEN RECEIVE IN EACH DAILY VITASAFE CAPSULE: [ingredient table]

ALSO AVAILABLE, A VITASAFE PLAN FOR WOMEN. CHECK COUPON IF DESIRED

Posed by professional models

To prove to you the remarkable advantages of the Vitasafe Plan... we will send you, without charge, a 30-day free supply of high-potency VITASAFE C.F. CAPSULES so you can discover for yourself how much stronger, happier and peppier you may feel after a few days' trial! Just one of these capsules each day supplies your body with over *twice* the minimum adult daily requirements of Vitamins A, C, and D... *five times* the minimum adult daily requirement of Vitamin B-1 and the *full concentration* recommended by the Food and Nutrition Board of the National Research Council for the other four important vitamins! Each capsule contains the amazing Vitamin B-12 – one of the most remarkable nutrients science has yet discovered–a vitamin that actually helps strengthen your blood and nourish your body organs.

Glutamic Acid, an important protein constituent derived from natural wheat gluten, is also included in Vitasafe Capsules. And to top off this exclusive formula, each capsule now brings you an important dosage of Citrus Bioflavonoid. This formula is so complete it is available nowhere else at this price!

WHY YOU MAY NEED THESE SAFE HIGH-POTENCY CAPSULES

As your own doctor will tell you, scientists have discovered that not only is a daily minimum of vitamins and minerals, in one form or another, absolutely indispensable for proper health... but some people actually need *more* than the average daily requirements established by the Food and Nutrition Board of the National Research Council. If you are a normally healthy person, but tire easily... if you work under pressure, subject to the stress of travel, worry and other strains, with resulting improper eating habits... then you may be one of the people who needs this extra supply of vitamins. In that case, VITASAFE C.F. CAPSULES may be "just what the doctor ordered" – because they contain *the most frequently recommended food supplement formula for people in this category!*

POTENCY AND PURITY GUARANTEED

There is no mystery to vitamin potency. As you probably know, the U.S. Government strictly controls each vitamin manufacturer and requires the exact quantity of each vitamin and mineral to be clearly stated on the label. This means that the purity of each ingredient, and the sanitary conditions of manufacture are carefully controlled for your protection! When you use VITASAFE C.F. CAPSULES you can be sure you're getting exactly what the label states... pure ingredients whose beneficial effects have been proven time and again!

HOW AMAZING PLAN SLASHES VITAMIN PRICES

With your free 30-day supply of Vitasafe High-Potency Capsules you will also receive complete details regarding the benefits of an amazing new Plan that provides you regularly with all the factory-fresh vitamins and minerals you will need. By participating in the Vitasafe Plan now you are never under any obligation! When you have received your first 30-day trial supply, simply take one VITASAFE Capsule every day to prove that this formula can help you as it is helping so many others. But you remain the sole judge. If you are not completely satisfied, and do not wish to receive any additional vitamins, simply let us know by writing us before the next monthly shipment – or you can use the handy instruction card we will provide – and no future shipments will be sent. Yes, you are under no purchase obligation ever, you may cancel future shipments at any time!

But if you are delighted – as so many people already are – you don't do a thing and you will continue to receive fresh, additional shipments regularly every month – for just as long as you wish, automatically and on time – at the low Plan rate of only $2.78 plus a few cents shipping for each full month supply. You take no risk whatsoever – you may drop out of this Plan any time you wish without spending an extra penny, by simply notifying us of your decision a few days before your next monthly shipment. Take advantage of our generous offer! Mail coupon NOW.

A VITASAFE PLAN FOR WOMEN

Women may also suffer from lack of pep, energy and vitality due to nutritional deficiency. If there is such a lady in your house, you will do her a favor by bringing this announcement to her attention. Just have her check the "Women's Plan" box in the coupon.

Help yourself or someone you love to new health and happiness!
Mail Coupon Now

VITASAFE CORP.   47-H
43 West 61st Street, New York 23, N. Y.

Yes, I accept your generous no-risk offer under the Vitasafe Plan as advertised in Private-Eye.

Send me my FREE 30-day supply of high-potency Vitasafe Capsules as checked below:
☐ Men's Plan   ☐ Women's Plan
I ENCLOSE 25¢ PER PACKAGE for packing and postage.

Name _____

Address _____

City _____ Zone ____ State _____

This offer is limited to those who have never before taken advantage of this generous trial. Only one trial supply under each plan per family.

IN CANADA: 394 Symington Ave., Toronto 9, Ont.
(Canadian Formula adjusted to local conditions.)

Mail Coupon To **VITASAFE CORPORATION, 43 West 61st Street, New York 23, N. Y.**
or when in New York visit the VITASAFE PHARMACY, 1860 Broadway at Columbus Circle
© 1957 VITASAFE CORP.   IN CANADA: 394 Symington Ave., Toronto 9, Ontario   ® VITASAFE REG. T.M.

The Fiction House Press Men's Magazine Replica Line is available at
www.FictionHousePress.com

Be sure to check our website regularly as we are constantly adding more men's magazine replicas to our lineup.

Printed in the USA
CPSIA information can be obtained
at www.ICGtesting.com
LVHW080154020524
779119LV00011B/508